CENSUS

Armida Publications is a founding member
of the Association of Cypriot Book Publishers,
a member of the Independent Publishers Guild (UK),
and a member of the Independent Book Publishers Association (USA)

www.armidabooks.com | Great Literature. One Book At A Time.

Summary:
Set in the middle of the twentieth century in the mountainous Cypriot village of Spilia, denoting "Cave"
in Greek, *Census* follows the pregnancy of cancer patient Maria, who conceives during her single intercourse
with the angelically handsome young Michael, visiting from Patmos, the Aegean island of John's Revelation.
The gestation culminates in the "nativity" at a Nicosia clinic, of a bodiless, unseen Christ.

Though incorporeal, scentless and colourless, the mysterious life-giving force that is liberated explosively from
Maria's womb, brings about premature efflorescence and a diffusion of aromas across the clinic's flower pots;
and akin to healing energy, it begins curing the spiritual and psychosomatic ailments of all those it overshadows,
urging the distinguished members of the island's medical community, present at the labour, to dedicate their life,
scientific knowledge and abilities to studying and utilizing this unknown new energy.

[1. General - Fiction 2. Literary - Fiction 3. Visionary & Metaphysical - Fiction
4. Christian - Classic & Allegory - Fiction 5. Occult & Supernatural - Fiction]

English translation by: Despina Pirketti

Editor: Helen Stavrou

Cover original artwork: *Girl with a Pearl Earring* by Johannes Vermeer

———•••———

Many thanks to the
Ministry of Education and Culture of the Republic of Cyprus
for financially supporting the translation of this work.

———•••———

Greek editions: 1st edition, 1973 • 2nd edition, 1991 • 3rd edition, November 2014

1st English edition: June 2015

ISBN-13 (paperback): 978-9963-255-30-6

CENSUS

a novel by

PANOS IOANNIDES

English translation by

Despina Pirketti

Edited by

Helen Stavrou

ARMIDA

——◦❦◦——

Dedicated to:

A.Chr., an astute guide upon rough terrain

Kl.I., a boundless source of knowledge and logos

K.H"G., a paradigm of prudence and tireless friendship

P.I.

——◦❦◦——

THEY CAUGHT SIGHT OF HIM BY THE CURVE OF THE road. Carrying a backpack and a guitar, he was walking uphill in the same direction they were driving. He didn't nod, nor did he turn to look as they drove past him; a few meters down the road, the driver's foot went for the brake pedal. The Deux Chevaux screeched and came to a stop.

The stranger paused and smiled at the passenger as she opened the door for him. He was young, twentyish; a foreigner, from Patmos. He had walked across the half of Mesa-Oria and was now heading for "Spiliā"; two friends of his, conservators of Byzantine wall-paintings in small churches of Soleā and Marathasā, were to put him up for a few days. No, he was not a painter or a conservator of icons, nor was he a musician; he was just a visitor.

"We too are headed for Spilia… What a coincidence, eh? By the way, it's Spilia, with the accent on the –i! We're staying for a few days, to rest. I'm sorry – I'm Maria Akritas. This is my husband, Joseph Akritas".

"Michael".

Joseph Akritas glanced at him nonchalantly through the rear-view mirror, nodded his head vaguely and turned his focus back to the road.

"And the region is pronounced Soléa and Marathāsa. But the way you said it is more fine-sounding" Maria Akritas said.

"Only what's authentic is fine-sounding" commented the young man.

Then there came a gust of wind; the elm trees on the floor of the valley started to rustle.

"And I'm not going there to rest".

Maria Akritas looked at him awkwardly, not knowing what to say; she let out an "Oh" and smiled.

The stranger held the guitar, gliding his fingertips over it. The music merged with the motor's buzz. Maria Akritas turned her head backwards to face him. He was tall, blond, with straight, shoulder-length hair, lightly touching his leather jacket that was garnered with fleece. A synaeresis of masculinity and femininity; only his sparse beard revealed his gender – a beard that was almost fluff – and his voice:

"May I?"

"Of course you may! We adore music, especially Greek music. What is it you play?"

She spoke as if she knew him from far back, this maladjusted, bitter woman! From the moment he smiled at her, sitting inside the car with ease, she felt loose and euphoric.

"It's not Greek music".

"Then what is it?"

"Just music".

She smiled a smile that was not contagious, so she kept quiet. Joseph Akritas kept looking at the street, emotionless.

"I used to do some singing myself, professionally! Or, rather, as an amateur", she felt the need to revise.

"You can't be Cypriot, Maria", he said.

More than the "can't be", she was mindful of his casual address – Maria.

"Just by half; my father was Cypriot, my mother was Egyptian, a

Copt. I was born in Amman. Joseph here I met in Barcelona. He's a journalist, a cameraman, a war correspondent — you know, a Jack of all trades! And a very adept one too. Joseph Akritas! He was there for a story, the atomic bomb that sank in the Mediterranean, you remember; and instead of the bomb, he dug me up!"

Joseph Akritas turned her way. She didn't see his gaze but she felt its rigidity. And with a grimace of submission, she changed the subject:

"Is it a beautiful island? Patmos!"

"It's my island".

She asked him how it was he decided to travel in mid-winter. Cyprus is nice in the summer; or spring. Or, as a mocking local poet says, "in the darkness". And journeys become more comfortable, especially up in the mountains.

"Now is always the best time" he replied.

She felt his gaze caressing her.

"You're beautiful" he told her and carried on playing the guitar.

Joseph Akritas restrained himself from reacting; he pretended either not to have heard or that the phrase was an unfinished line from a song. And he remembered that this simple two-word statement was exactly what he had wanted to tell her when they had first met, but he hadn't dared; instead, he had spoken of a journalist's "missionary" work.

On her part, flattered from what she heard and grateful for the other's silence, she turned ahead, sank into her seat and surrendered herself to an unanticipated bliss.

The car left the main road and with a bump entered the snaking street that led to "Spilia-Kourdali" as indicated by the bilingual street sign at the turn. The carrosserie of the Deux-Chevaux shuddered from head to toe; for a moment or two, fingers jumped recklessly on the steering wheel as well as on the guitar strings.

"This road does not lend itself to... to music" she said, without turning her head back. "It goes on like this until Spilia. But it's so picturesque, especially the first kilometres. In the summer, at dawn or before dusk, I like to walk here, all the way up the road".

Orchards became denser, and the street, for approximately one kilometre, turned into a spiral. The Deux-Chevaux squeaked maniacally; at the turn, down the road from the village's first houses, a big, broken plane tree branch was blocking the way. Joseph Akritas sharply stepped on the brakes, put the car into neutral and got out. The young man followed him. They removed the obstacle, in silence, and faced one another for the first time. The young man's eyes were cyan blue; Joseph Akritas' a washed-out brown colour, sank into two cold crevices below a forehead dichotomized by two wrinkles, as deep as knife wounds. He was around thirty five but he looked fifty. She wasn't older than twenty-five. The two of them were separated by ten years and a crop of wrinkles that was rather large for someone his age. Her concealed despair made them coeval.

"Thank you", Joseph Akritas said.

It was the first time he spoke. Voice broken just like his face.

"Patmos is one of the islands I haven't visited. Perhaps some-day... Patmos and Cythera. Though I'm in no position to benefit from either".

"Your job must have taken you..."

"...everywhere it shouldn't have", Joseph Akritas cut in on him.

"We usually go where we should".

The young man was right. Akritas was annoyed. He felt the need to retort; for what he'd said to his wife a moment ago too, as if he wasn't even there, as if he wasn't...

"Why do you speak like that?" He wanted to ask about the casual address, but he chose not to.

"If you prefer, sir..."

Though not ironic in tone, the "sir" sounded like irony.

They went back to the car.

"Aren't you freezing?" she asked, content with the conversation she had observed behind the window, without actually hearing it.

And when the car continued its course:

"I'm freezing... Aren't you? I do hope Avgi remembered to have the *tsiminia* mended. *Tsiminia* – that's fireplace in these parts. Avgi is a friend of ours, she's the school teacher. Each time Joseph emigrates here for a while, she puts us up. Say, where are your friends staying?"

"I don't know. I'll find them".

"Have they been in Cyprus long?"

"It'll be two years in two months".

"And they work with wall-paintings?"

"They've restored two chapels; it will take them an additional nine months to complete the third".

"Greeks?"

"No. He's Russian, from Crimea. She's Jewish, Alexandrian".

"And they worked in Patmos?"

"No. I met Piotr and Hanna Archangielsk on a fishing boat, travelling to Matala".

"Can they speak Greek?"

"They can. Among six languages".

"What about you?"

"Seven".

"Already? So young?"

"What about you, Maria?"

"Greek and Arabic. I'm not much of a polyglot. As opposed to Joseph. He definitely doesn't fall short. He can speak three languages fluently, and studies another two, when he has time. How did you learn to speak so many languages? At university? Or was it... through sleep-learning?" she joked.

"Sleeplessness!" he reciprocated the joke. "Relatively easy; I live them in their cradles".

"In the countries where they are spoken? You must be travelling all the time".

"It's not terrible".

"Of course not. As long as you're well-heeled, which certainly makes things simpler".

"Or frugal".

The Deux-Chevaux took a sudden turn before it exhaled, sliding along the downhill road. In the nick of time, a herd of goats sought refuge by the roadside. The young shepherd, brandishing his rod and cussing, had no time to recognize them.

"Mr Mathew's son", Maria Akritas said. And, turning to their co-traveller, she added: "Here we are!" and pointed to the houses in the village, penned in their lavish green narrowness. "She has probably been waiting for hours. We wrote we would be here earlier. We're late. The soup must be cold by now. You know what? You should come with us, have something warm. Then we'll take you to your friends".

"The gentleman must be tired", Joseph Akritas unexpectedly intervened.

"Not at all", replied the youth. Then: "But not tonight. I'll take a rain check on that".

He saw Maria's disparaging look and her husband's neutral expression and he smiled, picking up the guitar and backpack.

"To the coffee-shop, please", he said.

"Just for a soup! It's really no trouble ..." the young woman repeated with obvious disappointment.

"Thank you. I need to be at the Archangielsks at six".

"What if... you hadn't hitched a ride? Cars are quite rare in these parts, this time of the year".

"Then they wouldn't be expecting me at six".

When the car overtook him, the mountain side along with Spilia vanished in a blinding sulphurous glow. He stepped on the brakes to stop the car. Rain came pouring down. Maria Akritas turned to look at the stranger; he'd disappeared.

"We should get out too. Until the weather clears".

"We're almost there".

And he started the engine. The wipers juddered on the windscreen. The second they wiped it clean, it was covered again in layers of rain, replete with sounds and bubbles. He drove on, guessing where the street was, using his handkerchief to wipe the fog of their breaths, glued to the glass, solidified. A dog, on the uphill path to the church, threw itself against the car, barking desperately. Kicking its legs, it leapt up onto the window beside her.

"It's Rex! Shall I open the door?"

He shrugged and slowed down. The dog along with a gush of wind and rain swept inside the car.

"Why do they keep pets if they are going to throw them out on the street?" she said to herself.

They parked at the fence gate. The rose bush and dahlias had been trampled by the wind; the young plane tree too. Windows and doors, hermetically closed. No light whatsoever. They looked at each other in bewilderment. That was a first. She had spoiled them, always standing at the door, waiting, the entire house lit up, the scent of *latzia* –quercus alnifolia – and *trahana soup* lingering as far as the street corner. The one time she hadn't welcomed them at the door was when an inspection had been scheduled and she had to stay at school – but even then she had opened the entire house for them and asked a neighbour to welcome them.

He honked; again, harder. There was no trace of life inside the house, or in the entire neighbourhood; only the dog growled, annoyed.

"Why don't we go in?" Maria Akritas said. "You do have a key".

He groped for it in the glove-box where he kept insurance papers and his driver's license; and found it.

He went on, without rushing, defying the rain, to the door. He opened it and hit the light switch. The glow brought out the wilderness, both in the house and outside. Maria Akritas pushed the dog aside and in two bounds it jumped into the sunroom where it began shaking off the rain, sprinkling the fleece carpet. She lifted the fur on her coat, tucked her head inside it and in small, quick steps squished through the mud puddles.

"We'll bring in the suitcase later", she told him on her way in. "Let's light the fire first".

"She left a note", Akritas said, and walked across the room to the chest.

Leaning against the vase with the juniper berry, a folded note awaited.

"What does it say?"

"Nothing... That there's food in the fridge and fruit and smoked ham in the pantry."

"Is that all?"

"That's all".

"Not where she went? Nothing else?"

"We'll find out. Soon enough".

"Can I see it?"

She held the note:

"I leave in a hurry. Will be away. Don't know for how long. The house is at your disposal for as long as you want it or forever. There's roast chicken in the fridge, fruit, groceries and smoked ham in the pantry. Farewell. Love you, Avgi".

"It's..." she began, but then stopped.

She slowly took off her coat and hung it on the portmanteau. Then, her muddy shoes. She picked them up and walked to the bedrooms. He sat in the high back rustic chair in the sunroom, made somewhat more comfortable by two thick embroidered cushions. The note he folded and left beside him, on the wooden carved chest; there, clusters of black and red grapes, sky blue birds, were slaughtered by the wood cracks.

When she returned, now in her bathrobe and slippers, she found him motionless in the same spot where she left him, absentmindedly patting the chest.

"Everything is in its place in her bedroom. If she took something, she did so hastily and… I do hope…"

"Enough, Maria. We'll find out".

"It's so strange. Almost terrifying. I can't make any sense out of the note she left for us. She left in a hurry, doesn't say where to or for how long, why she's going, and that creepy 'stay for as long as you like or forever', it makes me feel I'm inside the house of a… Like an heir or a burglar".

"I'm sure there is an explanation for everything, Maria".

"There isn't always, Joseph".

"I'm afraid there is", he replied, trying to conceal, albeit subtly, his own tormenting concerns.

"I'm cold".

Kyros Demetriades, Principal at the Spilia Elementary School, and father Stavros Alexandrinos, son of a wealthy cotton trader hailing from Spilia, though born and raised in Alexandria, Egypt, welcomed them cordially. Boisterous joy was expressed by all the guests at the coffee shop-and-butchery dubbed "Lovely Spilia" – of which there were few at that particular moment: the forest ranger, the centenarian grandpa Mathew and two workers at the Forestry Department, playing backgammon for their drinks. They all stood up and insisted on treating them to drinks. They exchanged compliments with all of them, promised to soon share their news and sat with the priest and the headmaster.

"What are you having?" asked Father Stavros. He then turned, and in stentorian voice, summoned Nicodemus who was busily chopping a sow in the kitchen.

The shopkeeper approached, wiping his huge hands on his apron.

"Welcome" he said, reaching his hand out. His palms were sticky, still warm with a layer of fat and blood, resisting the superficial wiping.

"Take their orders", Father Stavros ordered.

"Chamomile for me", Maria Akritas said.

"And Mr Akritas?"

"Cognac, please".

"With honey or sugar?"

"Honey", Maria Akritas replied. "Just a bit".

"When did you arrive?" Kyros Demetriades asked.

"This afternoon".

"I suppose Miss Avgi will put you up as always".

"Yes! As always. You do know that…"

Grandpa Mathew cut in on her, noisily dragging his chair towards them. He squeezed between the teacher and Akritas. The two of them moved their chairs to either side, making room for his cape and gumboots, and what little was left of him from his initial dimensions. He banged his worry beads onto the table. Nicodemus came back.

"A bottle of single-star cognac complete with meze", grandpa ordered.

"Impossible", Akritas protested. "We just ate".

"Bring it!" the old man bit back and sent the shop keeper away with a brusque gesture that made the beads rattle; they were made of amber, a gift, three years ago, by Akritas, a souvenir from Aqaba. At first, grandpa Mathew looked at them with scepticism, as though they heralded one more sign of his gradual decline. In time though he compromised, turning the string of beads into an extension of his fingers, "his wristwatch and pulse" according to Kyros Demetriades.

In the meantime, the forest ranger too moved his chair beside them. He was a short man, with a hypertrophic head, fluffy hair and a huge bump on the temple; he rarely talked, even more rarely laughed and never reported the – more than few – misdemeanours of his fellow villagers to the police. "Why should I give them a ticket?" he told his friend, the Police Sergeant. "Whether I give them one or not, neither will they conform nor will the Government keep its promises. So?"

"You still have the worry beads", Maria Akritas said.

Grandpa Mathew did not hear her; Demetriades repeated the question.

"As if there's anything left for us, teacher. Melanie took her knitting needles with her along with her stubbornness. I'll take my sins and this here".

Then he sank back.

"Of late we've lost all signs of you", Demetriades said. "It's been a while since we last saw your reports".

"Yes, as if peace has reigned on earth!" Father Stavros joked.

Maria Akritas looked at her husband, hoping that here, at the coffee-shop he wouldn't fall into one of his lapses, so common over the past few days. Her hopes went unheeded. Akritas had fixed his gaze on the beads, appearing oblivious to what was happening around him. She rushed to cover for him:

"Not yet, I'm afraid, Father Stavros! Joseph's silence does not always mean peace. No one's silence, I guess".

"Well, up here you are bound to get some rest", Demetriades said. "Willy-nilly… How long are you planning on staying?"

"Two or three days. Perhaps a week".

"Longer!" Akritas unexpectedly intervened.

"This is very nice", Father Stavros said.

"By all means", Demetriades assured them. And then: "Where did you travel lately? We lost track of you!"

"Where didn't he travel you should ask!" Maria Akritas replied vaguely on his behalf, anxious for an opportunity to ask what they knew about their friend and her whereabouts.

Nicodemus arrived with his tray. Then he shared out glasses and meze dishes: artichoke, lettuce hearts, salami, parched broad beans, bulgur wheat with lard, pork and snails. Then he opened the bottle, securing it between his knees. He pushed the teacup in front of Maria Akritas; the hue of honey glowed inside it.

"Cheers", exclaimed Father Stavros.

"Roast some sausages", the forest ranger told Nicodemus.

"But we've already eaten", Maria Akritas laughed.

The rural worker's answering look meant that he wouldn't take no for an answer.

By the time the rest of the meze dishes arrived, the remainder of the guests at "Lovely Spilia" had gathered around their table. Neither Joseph nor Maria were annoyed. They knew that, sooner or later, this would be the unavoidable outcome; that in the villages of Cyprus it is rude to leave guests and visitors by themselves, even if it is obvious that this is exactly what they long for.

"Was it you who drove the stranger to the village?" Father Stavros inquired, settling his sparse hair across his bald forehead.

"Yes", Maria Akritas replied. "He asked us to leave him here. I wonder if he's found the house".

"I took him", the priest said. "His friends, the ones he came to visit, are renting my upper floor. They are iconographers, conservators of icons".

"They've revealed a wall painting from the 11th century", Demetriades supplemented the information offered by the priest.

"I'd like to see it. If I'm allowed".

"Of course…" Demetriades began.

But he was interrupted by the priest:

"I would advise you against it, dear Maria. My tenants are mysterious people. When they're working, you don't exist. They'll neither welcome nor bid you farewell. Working in muteness— they didn't even offer me a glass of water. First time I felt like a stranger in the Lord's House! Never set foot there again".

"I myself go there from time to time", declared the Headmaster of the Elementary School. "I enjoy observing them, the manner in which they work. A proper rite! They're like neurosurgeons. They use their tools, tiny pincers and very small spatulas, to peel off gypsum layers; then, with their brushes and some cotton, they bring out the colours. Just a tiny bit each day! Sometimes it's less than an inch. Just recently it took them one and a half weeks to clear one eye of the Pantocrator!"

"What kind of people are they?" asked Maria Akritas.

"The happy kind!" the teacher replied in one word.

"Young, I suppose?"

"Over sixty... Maybe even eighty!"

"I thought... Judging from the young man, who said they were his friends".

"Personally I would think they're seventyish. But they look younger than me; and I'm not even forty".

"Forty-five..." the priest joked benignly.

"Come on, father, you're breaking confidentiality!" Demetriades smiled. "Let alone the fact that you're distorting it! We agreed on forty-four. Two years younger than you".

Everyone around them laughed, except for Joseph Akritas, who looked on absentmindedly.

"The stranger, is he their son?" the coffee-shop owner asked, serving the additional meze dishes.

"No", Father Stavros replied. "He's actually one of us. From the island of... He told me, but I forgot. And to think that the island is emblematic in relation to our religion. It's... Anyway".

"Patmos", Maria Akritas contributed.

"Yes, exactly", Father Stavros said and refilled the glasses. "The island of the Apocalypse". And he raised his glass: "So, it's great to have you here!"

"Great to be here!"

They took a sip.

"What about Avgi? Why hasn't the young teacher joined you? Or do the Jews dictate otherwise?" the priest asked, with a voice distinctly laced with irony.

"Didn't I mention it? I thought..." Demetriades muttered. "It appears she went to the city".

Maria Akritas readily seized the opportunity she'd been expecting for a while:

"Yes, precisely. She left a note saying she's away. But it wasn't very clear. Did she tell you where she was going?"

"No, nothing. I assumed she came to you, in Nicosia", Demetriades said.

"Without applying for a leave of absence? I should think that..." Maria Akritas went on.

"No, it's no longer necessary. Once you give notice of being indisposed, you are entitled to uncertified three-day leave".

"And she's been away since....?"

"Tuesday, yesterday. I believe she left on Monday afternoon".

"So, tomorrow..."

"Yes, she should normally be back tomorrow".

"The Archangielsks don't know either? I mean, she worked with them", Father Stavros remarked.

"As far as I know, no one does".

"How did she get to the city?" Maria Akritas insisted on asking.

"I don't know this either. I only heard she had been seen along the dirt forest road to Platania, on foot, a small suitcase in hand.

A young girl, a student of hers, saw her on Monday. At about five in the afternoon. That was the last we heard of her".

The pause underscored everyone's surprise and wonder – except for grandpa Mathew who, impartial to what transpired around him, suddenly took up a fight with his old lady, asking her to move over in bed. Then, as suddenly as he had erupted, he fell back into silence.

"Grandpa finally snuggled down!" Nicodemus laughed.

Maria Akritas finished her tea and asked, trying to do so in a voice that was calm and natural:

"How has she been of late? It's been two months since we last saw her".

"Just fine! She looked well on Monday. Cheerful, as usual".

"Her note said nothing as to where she was going or why; we were truly worried".

"I don't understand", Father Stavros said. "And you of all people!" he turned to Demetriades. "You said nothing. I could have taken care of it".

Joseph Akritas lifted his gaze from the amber beads and fixed it on Father Stavros. The priest tried to decode the meaning of that look; in vain. In Akritas' eyes he discerned unjustified cruelty and rebuke. He wanted to disarm him with his innocence, or whatever he thought of as his innocence, with a gesture that suggested he had no part in what had happened; but he failed and lowered his eyes. He took a piece of sausage and shoved it in his mouth, chewing on it with his golden dentures; lard leaked out, spraying his palate and lips.

"I'll settle down here", Joseph Akritas spoke for the first time in a while, obviously following his own connotations or belatedly

replying to some of the questions posed earlier by the gathering.
"I'll buy a house, I'll renovate it and then I'll try to…"

Maria Akritas looked at him in astonishment she couldn't conceal; this was the first time since the day she had picked him up
at the airport, that he offered an indication, albeit minimum and
vague and untimely, of his true intentions. Apart from the typical
stuff, he had said nothing, neither to her nor to his friends who
had rushed to welcome him; nor, for that matter, to the English
editor-in-chief of the World News Agency who flew from London in order to get a first-hand briefing on what was happening to him. Joseph gave no explanation for his elongated silence.
The offer of a new mission in war-stricken Indochina, which in
the past he would have gladly taken on in anticipation of further
achievements, he rejected. In light of this inexplicable refusal of
his, the editor-in-chief announced that the Board of the Agency
would review his overall stance, which "equalled a refusal to per-
form his duty!" In fact, they had failed to convince him, despite
covert threats by the Agency's legal advisor, to surrender the material he had compiled in Africa and Asia — which had cost the
Agency a fortune! There was no reference on his part, no clue
or indication of his experiences or the decisions that Maria felt
he had taken. Only now, ten whole days after his return, at the
coffee-shop, in the context of a slightly relevant conversation!,
did he state what he intended and what he would try to do…
But not why.

"This is marvellous!" Father Stavros exclaimed. "Isn't it, teacher?"

Demetriades was of a different opinion. One he didn't care to
hide. A cosmopolitan, a well-travelled man, he said, couldn't
possibly consider settling down in Spilia. Life in the village might
be fine for him, a man whose diffidence in claiming promotion
and transfer had him metamorphosed into a pot-bellied missionary of Elementary Education; and for the vicar too, a herd of

children and grandchildren along with a fortune tied to his rod; for the Archangielsks, who found serenity in chapels and monasteries, digging up Byzantine mysticism; but not for a veteran journalist, at the peak of his career, a man who had managed to grasp and measure with his very hands the pulse of contemporary life, a witness and translator of two decades of splitting...

"The atom", Nicodemus naively offered.

Everyone, except for the Akritases and grandpa Matthew, laughed.

Demetriades rounded up his homily with an observation that made Maria Akritas want to kiss him.

"After all, there's one more thing; Maria! I doubt if Maria, in spite of her love for our village, would be willing to share in our misery. What do you say, dear Maria?"

"I don't know what to say..." she hesitated. "It depends... on so many things".

Nicodemus, still upset over his slip of tongue, took a sudden last sip of his drink and stood up.

"Shall I put on the News?" he proposed.

"Sit tight" the priest rebuked him. "What for?"

"They're always mumbling the same things", some other guest muttered.

But all of a sudden, Father Stavros had a change of heart:

"Come to think of it, switch the darn thing on; let's hear about the weather. I'll have workers on the roof tomorrow and I shudder at the thought of having to postpone".

"The way things are going this year..."

The buzz of the broadcaster's voice filled the "Lovely Spilia". He said what they expected to hear, what they had been accustomed to hearing ever since the radio was placed here at the coffee shop, between pictures of Greek heroes from 1821 and National Martyr Kyprianos.

When Nicodemus got up and switched it off, music was heard, as they expected, from across the street: guitar music; unlike what they expected. They lifted their eyes to the upper floor, at the edge of the square; it was lit with yellow and blue light, and behind the curtains one could vaguely see the strangers. Every evening, at this hour, guests at the coffee-shop listened to the music played by the woman on an antique harpsichord. At first, the monotony of Bach and Scarlatti would enervate them; then they got used to it and learned to tolerate it; in fact, lately, most of them would whistle the tune as they played a game of hara-kiri or billiards.

"Man can get used to anything", Father Stavros had complained at the time.

But, today, the harpsichord was quiet; and the guitar played something other than Bach, something unknown and profound, piercing, something that cut through their very core like a chill.

Steaming, she walked out of the bathtub and stood in front of the mirror. Her eyes drained from crying, misty; her nipples and the whole of her tan body yearning to be touched. She dragged her fingers over the white line carved by the scalpel. Just like the stranger had strummed on the guitar string yesterday; hers, this string here, did not reverberate melodiously.

Six whole months had passed since the last time they made love; from the night before he left on his penultimate journey. He had

assured her, as he did on any other night before they were separated, that he would miss her, that where he was going only cruelty, barbarity and deprivation awaited him. On that same night,
after their unrestrained, wild coupling, while in the bath, she
had palpated the neoplasia for the first time and felt excruciating
pain. For an hour she'd stayed in the water, quivering and crying.
When she'd gotten out, she'd found him blissfully asleep; she
hadn't woken him up. The next day, on their way to the airport,
she chose not to say anything. She thought she'd first see a doctor
before upsetting him with the little she knew. Throughout the
course of his mission she never mentioned, either by phone or
in writing, the oncologist's diagnosis and the procedure she had
had to undergo. She didn't want to burden him with worry and
anxiety that would distract him from his exhaustive, dangerous
work on war fronts or maybe even make him cut it short and
return to Cyprus. She would let him know in due time. When
he came back without notice, five whole weeks before his scheduled return, he was unrecognizable, a wreck. By contrast to what
had occurred in the past, when each mission "enriched" him as
he put it, when he was eager to share with her his experiences
in regular letters he wrote each week, always on a Sunday, eager to share them with millions of readers and viewers across
the length and breadth of the planet, wherever the World News
Agency could reach, reporting with photographs and footage —
over the course of those two and a half months he had only sent
her three letters. Three laconic letters. He was fine, regularly
took aspirin and quinine, had frugal healthy meals, was in no
lethal danger. He reported as laconically. He spoke of everything
he always spoke of, but this time his words lacked his trademark
acrid, dramatic tone. His footage and photographs were now
the least overwhelming of all the news stories submitted to the
Agency for distribution and broadcast. He gave the impression
that he avoided stepping inside the eye of the cyclone, that he
observed events from a distance that afforded him a cold objec-

tive evaluation of the tragedy; that, more than the bullet that was fired, he was interested in the finger pressing the trigger; more than the finger, he was interested in the pretext and the intention. "What's wrong with you, Joseph?" the editor-in-chief had asked him. "You too, burnt out?" And this, to the man repeatedly honoured with international awards, one of which was specifically given for "the volumes of depravity and inhumanity he captures in a photograph, a frame, a face, a grimace".

She waited for a few days after his homecoming; and when she made sure he had no intention of asking her about herself, of giving her the opportunity to confide the horror that transpired inside her, she chose to launch an attack. She asked him first, what was wrong, how, when, where and why he had changed, if she could help in any way. She did so in the hope that, to avoid talking about his own issues, he would ask about her instead. He replied succinctly. He was fine, hadn't changed, it was just that who he always was had finally risen to the surface. Now, all he wanted to do was "spend" a few days in Spilia.

She followed his lead, letting him have his own way without intervening. Worrying in silence, she watched him.

He took lethargic naps that, with the exception of a few one or two-hour breaks, lasted for days on end. He exhausted himself hiking; he climbed every crest in the neighbourhood, read crime novels, light magazines, listened to music, enjoyed sitting by the fire and said he was now well-rested and relieved. But the rapport they had always had, since their first night in Barcelona — well, she might as well admit it, had expired. There was no confession, no nightmare at night, no waking him up and throwing her arms around him, to have him talk to her, or allow her to put him to sleep through the erotic languor they both used to seek in order to heal.

Not even when he had left for his recent journey to Africa and Asia which was to last several months did he ask her "to come near him". Not when he came back; the alienation that began with his previous journey now deepened. And what was left to remind her of the man she knew, or thought she knew, was his yearning to come to the village, and the love — though not as manifest as before — he still felt for Avgi. Had she not known Avgi for years, had she not loved her as much as he did, she would be suspicious and envious; but no, Avgi was above suspicion. The sister of a friend the British executed by hanging in 1956, during the struggle for liberation, orphaned in her infancy after the loss of her mother, Avgi was practically his younger sister. Since her brother's death, when she was twelve, he had stood by her throughout the course of her studies, he had her enrolled at the Teachers College, looked after her, smothered her like a brother and a friend. Avgi and Maria were only two years apart, joined by a wealth of what they had in common: their love for travelling, music, dance, sports. "And Joseph!" they often joked.

That's why Maria wasn't bitter about the fact that, for two days now, since Thursday when they came to Spilia, the only interest he showed was exclusively in tracking down their friend, his only activity driving back and forth to Nicosia, Limassol, Paphos, where Avgi had relatives, in quest of information; albeit unsuccessfully. He tried everything, asked for the help of common acquaintances and friends, went to the Ministry, the Police.

"Unless she ran away with a young man and now they're hiding", he told her yesterday.

"I wish it were that", she replied. "But it doesn't look like it".

"Why?"

"I would have known; it's not something you can hide. Or..."

"What?"

"Nothing. I was just thinking of the so many things we never share, things nobody puts into words; never and for no one".

She was right! There are so many things you never put into words for anyone; things you can't even confess to your own self.

Joseph! The things he held back from her! How many debaucheries within him, constantly, mutely, either softly or violently, since that fatal hour? Why now? The moment he attained his self-definition he is still unable to isolate in time, no matter how hard he strives for it, to achieve self-recognition that will once more enable him to help or be helped.

Maria! The desire, the longing she concealed within her, that affluence of love! God, how much she yearned for this erratic love to solidify around a seed, to sanctify, fertilize and heal her wounded insides!

Michael! His fingers revealing the apocrypha of sounds! If only he was as cognizant of the secrets of speech! How many mysteries would then be resolved! What profound and novel sentiment had the young man from Patmos awakened within her!

The dog! They picked it up from the alley on Thursday, its eyes

brimming with dedication and fear. There it goes again, growl-
ing. Where? Why? She got up in a rush to find it when she realized she was naked; a chill ran along her skin. She looked at her
body once again; the fuzz on her arms had roughened. She put
on her bathrobe, added wood to the water boiler to make sure
he would find hot water on his return, and walked to the front
door. The snow was already a foot high! The dog yapped happily at her, went inside and shook his white cloak of fur in the
sunroom. Some kids from the neighbourhood, faces burrowed
in their hand-knitted hoods brow-deep, were playing with the
snow. She stayed there, looking. One of them, the eldest, Micha-
lakis, saw her.

"Hello, Ms Akritas".

The other two boys did not greet her, nor did they respond to
her maternal nod. They just scattered, eyes lowered.

"Welcome, ma'am", the boy resumed, overcoming his hesitation,
and once he said it he ran to join his friends in relief.

"Thank you, Michael".

She unset the table and took the servings to the kitchen. She
intended to wash them, but she put it off; she'd rather do it tomorrow. For the whole of the afternoon her heart raced, she was
irritated. She took a sedative from her bag, gulped it down with
water and went back to the living room.

She sat, legs crossed, on the handmade carpet of colourful rags,
next to the fire; and started reading. It reminded her of something, this thin and leather-bound book, but she couldn't remember what it was. She casually picked up a magazine, browsed
through it, tried to solve a crossword puzzle: commercial street

in Athens, a metaphor, reversed, a form of medicine, *r* being the third letter... she jolted upright, the day's weariness weighing upon her eyelids. She stretched her back and crawled near him; then sat beside him, on the floor.

"What are you reading?"

"Nothing".

"Can I see?"

"It's just a book of essays".

"May I?"

He unwillingly handed it to her.

"Is it interesting?"

He nodded something between "I'm not sure" and "I suppose" — she couldn't tell. This man who, until recently would take advantage of a similar, even less keen question, to launch an exhaustive in-depth critique and analysis that would render reading the book redundant. And, quite often, less interesting!

She opened it to where he had placed the bookmark:

"And even more tragic is the last ascertainment of contemporary Theseus. No matter how hard he seeks for the Minotaur in the labyrinth, he is not going to confront him; alas, he won't be given the opportunity to fight and if need be fall heroically for his ideals, just as so many generations of Theseuses before him. Unfortunately, contemporary labyrinths, just as the labyrinths of each and every era, hide no monsters or other such fine and romantic stimulants we construe to fill the void within us. And when the epic element and the sacred aim vanish from our life, when we realize that our heroism and whatever it was that triggered it

were nothing but an illusion we ourselves had joined together out of shattered dreams and ideals of ours, then we begin, aged but now enlightened, in the darkness, to roll back the thread so as to return to the outer light, to the true and regrettably sole tangible sun in life, to sink back into the reality that awaits us beyond our walls. Better than the void we have known is the void plus the shell of the void. And so we move along, step by step, bit by bit, to crawl into the grave, to rot in peace next to the relics of Ariadne who once offered us the only life there is, and love, the only love there is, but we opted for the thread..."

She closed the book.

"Do you believe in this stuff?"

"Does it matter?"

"Of course it does! I mean, it's obvious you too, in your own way, are going through what it describes. And next to you Ariadne is rotting, according to the book".

He didn't reply immediately; he stoked the ashes and sat upright. Then:

"I don't know! Sometimes I wish it's exactly as the book says. Other times, this very thought makes me sweat."

"You used to be different, you believed in what you did; you were happy, doing what you trusted and loved, unearthing the unhappiness of others. Why have you pondered on your own unhappiness? That of the others' has not been eradicated yet. Or has it?"

"Can I have my book?"

"I'm sorry".

She gave him the book and stood up. If she hadn't imposed on herself the habit to love him and justify anything he did or said, she would have told him many things that would hurt and humble him, as he deserved. But, once more, she chose to rouse the connotations of her old feelings; to restrain herself.

"If I'm not mistaken, it was a gift from me, just before... no, a bit after our wedding. This book along with some others".

"It's the only one left overlooked; it was so small, I never had much regard for it..."

And he fell silent.

"I'm going to bed", she told him. "Shall I wait for you?"

"I'll sit for a bit longer".

"Goodnight. Don't forget the doors and taps. The dog too".

He checked the doors, tightened the taps and emptied the can into the dog's bowl. Just as he had done yesterday and the day before that, on Friday, and Thursday. Just as he's going to do tomorrow and the day after tomorrow, on Saturday and Sunday. "Goodnight, Ariadne!" She was lonesome, longed for him, and he unwilling to help. Neutral and a stranger.

"Goodnight".

He unlocked his case in silence, just like he'd done yesterday and the day before that, like he'd do tomorrow, lest he catch her attention and lose this small, secret private adventure. He browsed over the content like he always did, randomly picked up a few pages and read them, whilst correcting or deleting words here and there: *"And then hunger"*. Hunger. Or should I write hungriness? *"Heat"*. Infectious. Or something of the sort. I'll find it.

The proper adjective usually comes uninvited, or after you've grasped the nature of a specific situation. *"A riff over the camp of the South African captives that brought despair and the wish for an ending"*. Melodramatic and overstated. Just as the entire text. He needs to expose it, the truth has no need for concealment, only grit; or, if he dared, only… No! These texts and the piles of photographs and film footage he still hadn't developed and perhaps never would, those hundreds of exclusives that earned him fame and riches should not be offered as food to be consumed by the ravenous audience of the mass media. This, and he always knew it, was just a shell, the surface; the yolk underneath it had gone bad; the truth in the core was poison he was never allowed to divulge.

The new unpublished material inside his case, which they were now pressing him to deliver in order to be "put to use", would add greatly to the guilty misguidance of public opinion for which he definitely had a share of responsibility. His mentors would smother him with pay checks and covered expenses, after pouring it, unabridged and without commentary, into their hideous operation. He would tame them once more; have them eat from his palm. And they would lavishly offer whatever he required of them.

No, no, no he wouldn't! He would burn everything instead, put it in the blender, and do away with his "brilliant", "flourishing", "fantastic" professional past once and for all. Then, free at last, he would embark on the precarious plan he had conceived of, the operatic one; to seek the nirvana and those who live it in faith or knowledge or fear. Or stupidity! Or he would do something even simpler. How tentatively at the time, but how strongly now he meant what he had said the other day at the coffee shop! That he had decided to withdraw to Spilia. To buy a crumbling house, restore it and go away beyond reach, restore himself. Either on his own or with her. Tomorrow he would definitely let her know;

that she's free to either follow him or take her freedom into her own hands; she's young, beautiful, brimming with energy, health, it would be a crime to impose on her the life he had chosen for himself. Yes, tomorrow; he couldn't see why he should put it off. And if he hadn't done it in so many days now, it was because he didn't want to exacerbate her concern, his too, over the mysterious disappearance of their friend. But now he could see clearly that any further delay would be pointless.

Good! He locked the case.

He stole into the bedroom. She was asleep, one leg uncovered, naked on the yellow blanket; shapely, alluring, flushed. He stood there, looking at her, wondering how everything would be tomorrow at the same time, if what he had planned yesterday for today would take place tomorrow or the day after tomorrow, or if it would stagnate within his indecisiveness just like everything else inside and around him. He tucked her leg in and ensconced himself in his own bed, next to hers; in a place that was frozen.

She submerged herself beneath the foam from head to toe; teeth grinding in pain.

She was twenty five and condemned to die before reaching twenty six. Special surgeon, Dr Herodotou, director of the "Hygeia" Polyclinic, the man who examined her, was very clear: six, maybe nine months; a year, according to the most optimistic predictions.

"I only told you this because you insisted on asking. Most patients would rather not know".

"Will it be…?"

"Not necessarily; it depends. Fortunately, there are new means available".

During the time before she had found out for sure, when she only suspected what it was, her despair was greater. For the past three months, since she had undergone the first surgical procedure, her real time had become a viscous substance that was polluted; and despite the assurances of their elderly family physician that "there was no risk of a remission", that "she was more likely to die of a cold rather than this…", she couldn't shake off her initial fright; a dark cloud engulfed her mind and within it she lived and moved about and existed … At night she would jump out of her sleep drenched in sweat, breathless; she would run to the toilet to throw up or throw wide-open windows and doors and breathe in greedily. In the mornings she would take long hikes to exhaustion, imposing on herself the conviction that exercise on the one hand and spiritual clarity on the other, would give her body the physical immunity or defensive ability she urgently and utterly needed to oxidize it with health. Part of this makeshift defence programme was complete abstention from meat and its by-products. She was obsessed with the idea that animal toxins, products of an animal's last fright, would worsen her condition. After having drawn up this improvised line of defence that lay, and she knew it, within the limits of self-delusion and absurdity, she felt less vulnerable and closer to the physical wellbeing that would rescue her at the eleventh hour.

And when she later gradually regained, at intervals, a seeming balance and a pace of life that was more regular, she absolutely loathed the thought of undergoing a second check-up. More than the disease itself, she was afraid of the knowledge of the disease and the decision she would again have to take: that she couldn't be the exception to the rule. And she would have insisted till the end too, if, on Sunday night, sometime after she returned from a visit to Father Stavros, she hadn't been immobilized by a fainting spell–her eyes fluttering in a torrent of absolute colours and absolute darkness. She had fallen flat on the paved road, amidst the firethorn. She was not aware of how long she had lost consciousness; she only remembered waking up in excruciating pain. She crawled to bed and lay awake, sweating profusely, feeling sick – which every now and then would drive her to the sink only to vomit coughs and groans; and not even a drop of fluid, to sooth her. He was away in the city, in search and quest of the other woman. She rarely needed him and never, at moments like this, was he available, by her side. On that night, Sunday going on Monday, she decided the time had come for another visit to the surgeon. She would go the following day, before his return to the village. But even if he did come back before she left, she would offer no explanation; nor would she ask for his support, trained as she has been not to share her agony and pain; as if those two were the only things she exclusively owned, ever since she was a child. She learned to walk on her own, learned to read, write and do maths. On her own she had faced the panic of her first menstrual cycle, on her own she had chastised herself for every failure, for the whole lot of them, or enjoyed the unimportant victories; on her own had she walked into life and on her own had she... On her own she would depart! Yes, by now she dared say it and comment on it. She had nothing to hide, saw no reason to beat around the bush. It was quite simple, really; she would live for an additional nine months maximum; the time prescribed for pregnancy was also prescribed for submission. Then, at a peak, she would wane and surrender to what she was before the onset of remembrance. No reason for melodramas or new illusions to be hatched. She would go back to her seemingly normal life and if everything went according to the predictions, and if by then there was still no sign of the drug-panacea, in late June or early July she would pack a small bag and seek refuge at a good inexpensive clinic where she would be assisted to depart with the least possible agony. Yes, she had made up her mind; neither he nor her friends would know anything about it. She would invent a lie, put their suspicions, their worries, to sleep. Their suspicions. (They were obviously devoid of any worry.) Or she would leave in secrecy, giving a fake name and details to the clinic, to conceal her identity. Even after... if she was lucky, or 'if they were'.

After an exhausting, three-hour check-up, Mr Herodotou was laconic and clear: "No change, Ms Akritas. Whether this works for us or against us, time will tell. I want to see you again in three months, or, if an emergency presents itself".

Leaving the "Hygeia", dazed after everything she had suffered and the vagueness of what she had heard, she took refuge in a coffee-and-pastry shop; she sat at a remote table and ordered tea of mountain herbs and three varieties of chocolate cake. Three. The waiter checked her over in surprise and admiration. How can some people keep fit and elegant with such an appetite!

From the table next to hers, a young man was not able to keep his eyes off her. How could he have missed such a catch! She smiled at herself: "...it's in the eye of the beholder..." He attached to her smile the explanation that best suited him and waved to the waiter: "Spyros! Whatever the lady orders is on me".

He stood up and approached.

"Hello".

"Hello".

"I think we've met before. At the "Saturday Fever" disco? No? Then at the "Decision" boîte?"

"Nowhere!" she replied smiling. "I'm afraid I haven't had the pleasure".

"Your accent! You must be from Athens, right? Yes, I'm sure you... No? Well, anyhow, we've met now!"

"We haven't met yet".

"True! Let us meet then. May I?"

She nodded he could sit with her.

Her eagerness made him feel awkward. He took a seat, but his posture showed he was ready to get up and leave her undistracted with her desserts. He stole a few glances at customers around them, which fed their curiosity, and offered his hand to her:

"Nicos Phinikarides".

"Avgi Josephides" she replied and offered hers.

"From Limassol? Famagusta?"

"Nowhere. I mean... I come from so many places... you can't really pin me down".

"Then, let me rephrase. Where do you live? It can't be Nicosia, I'm sure I would have caught sight of you somewhere. Unless you moved here recently".

"I live in Spilia. I work there as a teacher".

"In Spilia! And where exactly is Spilia? Those people at the Education Office, banishing such teachers to Spilia! What's wrong with them?"

"Well, the provinces have their needs too!"

He watched as she devoured the desserts, one after the other. His remark he could no longer keep to himself:

"You must like sweets".

"I overdid it, maybe because I won't be paying for them. In any case, from time to time one is allowed self-indulgences. It's actually a must", she added.

"Of course, without it…"

She held her gaze upon him; he was dark, bulky, with velvety brown eyes… almost purplish. It was the first time she had seen eyes that bordered so close on red, and so… He wore a grenat pullover, velvet jeans with a huge buckle on the leather belt, and carried the arrogance of an irresistible heartbreaker. "Little does he suspect', she thought.

"How about… a short ride with my car? Once you're through with your self-indulging! To help you digest" – he combined the daring invitation with graceless humour.

'He's regaining his confidence, tasting the flavour of his success. I'm sure he thinks he's irresistible, that he's swayed me with his charm and humour. If only I told him what it is that makes me vulnerable… Though why? What for?'

"Why not?" she replied. "But I'm afraid there's no time. I'm supposed to take the rural bus in half an hour!"

"That's a shame", he said. "Then again… I can drive you. Where was it you said you live? Well?"

"Spilia-Kourdali. How about… the fare?"

"We'll negotiate on the way".

The driver of the red convertible Lotus wanted to collect his fare, without any negotiation and roughly after half an hour of

speeding recklessly at 120 km an hour, outside the deserted forest station in Platania. He drove the car into a clearing amidst
the immense age-long plane trees, switched off the engine in
silence, then moved along in his seat and, ignited, began kiss-
ing her mouth, neck and eyes, panting and repeating "I like you,
Avgi, I like you, I want you, I want you".

Embarrassed, with a feeling of pronounced guilt, she was overcome by the strong urge to surrender, to experience under the
weight of his firm pelvis and muscles everything Joseph had deprived her of for months; to forget, through cataclysmic pleasure,
the lethal threat that lurked inside her body. But just as quickly,
she shoved lust off with abomination. Welling up in defeated
complaint, she bowed her head down to her bosom and broke
out in sobs, as a flood of indecipherable sounds and unshaped
words flowed from within her.

The aroused man, astounded, withdrew his hands from her body,
pulled away in his seat, rolled down the window to breathe in a
gust of frozen wind and looked at her sideways, without a word.
Even though he had felt a strong impulse to slap her, throw her
out of the car, he gradually came to his senses, subdued the ferocious erection that tortured him and chose to apologize, amazed
at himself; had he so much as even imagined that the woman
he had picked up belonged to the pseudo-prudent, puritanical
genre of Cypriot women, he wouldn't have dared carry on.

He lit a cigarette, took a few deep, theatrical puffs, offered her
his silver cigarette case, and then, candidly, told her that what
had happened was her fault, it was she who encouraged him.

Maria, having regained her composure after her long cry, whispered he was right; she and what she was going through lately
were responsible for her hysterical outburst; and, yes, she would
like a cigarette now.

He looked at her without caring to comment on her apology. He chose a cassette and focused his attention on the music. In truth, he just pretended to listen. "Yellow river... yellow river... saffron water..."

This whole thing had left him flabbergasted. It was so unreal, as if... He took his place behind the steering wheel and stepped on the gas. Screeching, the Lotus sharply took the turn to Spilia-Kourdali.

Just outside the village, he suddenly and apparently without reason stepped on the brakes, took her hand in his and asked in a calm voice if he could see her again. He would like that; silly though it seemed to her, meeting her "had made a profound impression on him, if nothing else, it was original", he added jokingly.

"Well?" he asked again.

"I don't know. Perhaps! Let's leave it to chance".

"I'll come back", he declared.

"Why don't you give me your phone number? I'll call you".

"But, Avgi... Believe me".

"I have my reasons".

"Honestly, Avgi..."

"I lied to you. I'm married! And I'm not a teacher".

Outside the village cemetery they saw the two Archangielsks.

She knew it was them because they were accompanied by the youth from Patmos.

"Pull over... Can we drive them to the village?"

"There's not enough room", he said and hit the brakes.

The three strangers approached the car. She first, then Michael, made the introduction:

"Mr Phinikarides".

"Maria Akritas. Piotr and Hanna Archangielsk".

Only their bright white hair betrayed the Archangielsk's age. Their skin was seamless, eyes clear of any dark corners. Slim, tall, without pronounced marks of their gender on their body or face.

"Do get in, we can drive you. It'll be a bit crowded, but we'll manage", said the driver and opened the door.

"We'd rather walk", Piotr Archangielsk replied. Then, facing her, he added: "I'd be happy if you could visit some time; at the house or the chapel, at your own convenience".

"Gladly", she answered, taken aback by the unexpected invitation.

"We would like to talk to you", Hanna Archangielsk said.

"I'll come by as soon as I can", she replied to both of them at the same time.

"Who are they?" her escort asked when the three walked on some distance from the car.

"Archaeologists, Byzantinists, something like that. He's Russian, she's Jewish".

"And their son, what a handsome fellow!"

"Yes", she whispered and realized how poor words are to describe such youthfulness and beauty.

"So, neither Avgi Josephides, nor a teacher. Maria Akritas!" the Lotus driver thought aloud and drove on. "As you shall see from the visit card I put in your bag, I'm not... My name's neither Phinikarides, nor Nicos".

"I assumed as much".

"So, Maria Akritas. Wife of the well-known Joseph Akritas!"

"Who was that gentleman who drove you?" Joseph Akritas asked nonchalantly, the second the Lotus roared away from outside the gate causing jets of snow behind it. "Why didn't he come in?"

"He was in a hurry. Perhaps some other time. We met this afternoon, at a café, and he insisted on giving me a lift".

"You didn't mention you were going to Nicosia. Nor did you leave a note".

"I hope you weren't worried. What about you, what time did you get back?"

"Soon after you left, this morning".

"Anything new?"

"Nothing. Demetriades came by. If you're available tomorrow, he can take you to the chapel, to see what they're doing; and meet them, of course".

"I just did, a moment ago. Did he say when?"

"After twelve".

She went to the bedroom and put on her dressing gown.

"You obviously didn't go by the house", she said from inside the room.

"No".

She came back and offered him an envelope.

"I found this".

She gave him the letter. Express delivery prepaid and registered. He opened it with indifference, as if he already knew its content, read it; furtive sarcasm rekindled his eyes. Then he turned around and threw it in the flames.

"What was it?" she asked.

"Nothing".

"Is it about the reportage that's pending?"

"That they allege is pending".

"Don't you owe them an explanation?"

"None whatsoever! You, on the other hand, I do owe a few explanations to. I want us to talk about something important".

"I'm listening".

Just as quickly he changed his mind. "After your bath. Won't you take a bath today? I've drawn it for you. I'm going for a walk now. We'll talk tonight".

"Shall I wait for you before I eat?"

"'Might as well don't, I'm not hungry".

"If you agree, I'm thinking of inviting them for dinner on Saturday night. The three newcomers. Maybe some of the locals too".

"Do that", he said casually and went outside.

What was that expression she observed in his eyes? When, a minute ago, he had leant over and looked at her, she felt his gaze digging into her. Could he have known? What was he looking for? Did he finally suspect what she hid from him? Oh really now! What was she thinking? He couldn't get his mind off his own concerns.

She opened the tap and rinsed the suds off her body. In the sunroom she heard noise; now he was talking to someone in a low voice, almost whispering. Who was it? She tried to make out the speaker, but she couldn't. Yet she was certain they spoke of her.

For just a quick moment she felt the urge to run outside, astound them with the terrible truth and her nakedness, ignite their tenderness and pity. But no! That would be so childish, so unlike her character, her age, so against the right decision she made not to talk until he demanded she would.

She took off the shower cap, wrapped herself in the fluffy white bathrobe and sat down to get dressed. How frivolously she had treated that young, spoiled lad! What a cheap and easy way to offset your agony. Nevertheless, what had happened was flattering; it awoke feelings she had oppressed within her. Was he being honest when he said he wanted to see her again? Did he sense the fire simmering under the ice? Was it really worth taking the risk to call him? Oh, God of lust, how hollow does 'risk' sound in her case! His passionate embrace she so hypocritically repelled like some anaphrodisiac bourgeois, would perhaps be among the things that, in her dying moment, would flash before her eyes.

She smiled. What was she blubbering on about? There was no more credit or debit for her; she was left with nothing but the present, donated by means of a pharmaceutical micro-balance. But from within her plight she had discovered something positive; she was free. Her disease and Joseph's attitude had entitled her to live wherever and however she chose. Her flirtation with the bon viveur proved to her, though she hypocritically concealed it, how much she still sought self-assurance and passion; that if she wanted, from now on she could deplete her life without posting it to a ledger; get rid of every must and have to with a single swipe

The murmured conversation outside carried on; always about her.

"Who was it?" she asked when she got out of the bathroom.

"No one. Why?"

"You were talking. I heard you. With a man".

"Yes, it was no one".

She followed his gaze as it rested over the case where he enviously kept his manuscripts, his films, the tape recorder she had bought for him years ago.

At night, before dinner, as they sat by the fireplace, sipping chamomile tea they both enjoyed, he suddenly stood before her, ready to speak, but he immediately changed his mind and put it off. It was then she discerned, in his persistent look, the same expression she had traced the other day in her own eyes, as she combed her hair in the mirror at the Polyclinic.

The panic of those who have seen the truth. Latent panic.

Was that what the Archangielsks had seen too? Is that why they wanted to talk to her? And now Joseph — has he too arrived at a diagnosis? Has he finally suspected? Yes! There was no doubt about it. He had read her signal. He would offer his hand; though he hadn't let out any specific sentiment, she had no doubt that was why he had decided to talk to her.

On the same night, on his return from his regular two-hour hike, he found her sitting at the table in front of a glass of milk, her serving untouched. He sat with her, to keep her company. He wasn't hungry, though he hadn't eaten anything since lunch. He just helped himself to a glass of cognac and served some freshly squeezed grape juice from the kitchen for her. They talked about unimportant things; about the lawn, their neighbours in Nicosia adding one more storey to their house, the weather, grandpa Matthew who had fallen into a coma. Then they went back to the fireplace. Outside, snow kept falling; the radio said it had reached two feet in the semi-mountainous areas, one meter in Troodos square. If the weather kept on like that, in a few days they would be cut off in the village.

With a burning coal he lit his pipe:

"I met them too", he said, inhaling smoke; the glow penetrated his eyes. "I was passing by and the young man invited me in. It was the first time I saw a living room furnished with anything you can imagine, except for furniture. There was a carpet, a few stools, magazines and maps. And the fire! They were cooking corn-on-the-cob in the fire; olives too. With butter and salt. And there was this wine he himself makes…"

He fell silent for a while, then moved the logs with the trident and went on:

"They are enchanted with a face, a head; it's bodiless, hovering self-sustained, seemingly irrelevant to the rest of the wall-painting. Very interesting! I saw it in their replication-book. That's what they call it. Whatever they restore, they draw in that exercise book. The replication, they actually call it reversal!"

She looked him in the eyes; yes, he was calmer tonight. Now she could attempt to ask him herself, to push him — albeit with an ulterior motive — taking a step towards her own confession. In spite of her latest decisions, she was yearning to share it with someone, anyone. Him, first and foremost!

"You were saying something this afternoon", she told him.

"Yes. I want you to know that what I said at the coffee shop the other day, I meant; I presumed that in the meantime you realized that. Perhaps the only thing you didn't understand was that what I said was exclusively intended for me; I'm not so selfish to want you to accompany me to the stake".

There was a self-indulgent, hopeful irony in his tone; a reverberation of his old self. Perhaps this was only the beginning.

"About that... it's good we don't know who will accompany who".

"No one accompanies anyone!"

"Do you really believe that?"

"Yes. It's one of the few things I do believe".

"Why? What's the reason?"

"For a thousand reasons. It's self-evident, this is how it is, how it's supposed to be, I only just realized myself".

"Whatever has happened over the last months..."

"It doesn't matter when and in what circumstances", he interrupted her. Isn't it enough that, unfortunately, it finally happened?"

"Perhaps we could... help each other. Perhaps there's a..."

"I won't accept it, Maria. No way. The only thing I'm still in a position to do, the only act of altruism, definitely my last one, is to help you see how pointless it is to waste your life with me, to live next to a dead body. It's irrational and unhealthy. Death is the most finalized divorce; in this sense, you are free; divorced. You have no moral or other obligation to me".

As if hypnotized, she stood up without offering any comments, emptied a can of food into the dog's bowl, checked the doors one after the other, checked the taps, and went back to the fireplace. She sat on the wooden stool. Her eyes were burning, she was holding back an ardent desire to scream that he had no right to abandon her, especially now, that he was being an egotist within the safety provided by his pain, that for God's sake they both knew from experience that they were not given pain in order to become dehumanized, but to...

She didn't, of course. She was lessened in front of the fire. She remembered her mother, why? She had barely known her; and they were lost, both she and the father she can no longer revive neither as a body nor with her feelings. He perished on the Palestinian front; or in the desert; from a bullet or hunger. Her mother too, searching for her youngest child – he had gone outside to play just before the sound of the... she ran outside calling his name and never came back. That voice stayed behind. And of five siblings, only her. Then, her adolescence, marked by two unfulfilled dreams; of a full plate of food and a dress in her own size. Her first song, out of tune and without rhythm, in front of soldiers dazed by rum and tropical heat, listening dispassionately whilst chewing gum or biting their dirty nails, and only every once in a while, at the chorus, when she lifted her dress to reveal her red panties, would they wake up. The singing contract at that *café chantant* in Cairo, she had signed with her whole body in a dressing room that reeked of hashish and sweat. Then the journey from Marseilles to Barcelona, with that Italian Jew impresario she thought she loved; in Malaga he was arraigned for smuggling opium. And then him ... exuding haughtiness for his talent and the power it afforded him. Absolutely certain he was in a position to change the world! Young, in his thirties, eyes flooded with irony and light, his entire being a string of optimism as he declared conceitedly that the world had broken down only for him to mend it! The "ever-moving" – as introduced to her by his colleagues. "The reporter that won't take no for an answer", he offered his own credentials. On the same night he proved to her he meant everything he had said, that he had fallen in love with her and he wanted her, as of that very night, in his bed.

And now... five years later. His demise she would understand if it ate away at a man of sixty, even fifty years of age, she would acknowledge it if it had appeared gradually. But how could it manifest itself in the span of a few months?

'In the span of a few days! Often within a moment! Just a single... Why am I surprised, God? What's wrong with me? Since the day I was born I've been diving head first into the grave'.

She fell into a sleep she had neither wanted nor pursued, on the low divan by the fire. Just before daybreak she dreamed of a head, without a trunk or neck, in a labyrinthine construction encircled by rays, sleek and sharp, forming a cross. At a slow pace first, then all the more quickly and with all her might, she began hunting it; it either kept drawing away or no, it was she herself who was walking on the spot, never actually moving an inch from her original position. As though she was submerged in sand. Then suddenly she stopped, as if taken by a revelation, she realised the vanity of the fight; surrendering to the vortex, she started to cry. When she felt both empty and satiated, she looked around her. The head hovered above her. Almost touching her. But the rays were no longer sleek, metallic. They merged into a warm radiance that made her soul sweat. And the head, it was no longer an infant's head as she had first suspected. It was the head of the stranger, the angelic head of the young man from Patmos, smiling at her as it grew bigger and plunged into the void like a meteorite.

In the morning, over breakfast, he told her he had heard her crying the previous night. Late in the afternoon, when he returned from his evening walk, he rephrased: he said she hadn't only been crying at night, she had also been laughing in her sleep, and that she had been immersed in a bliss he had never before seen on her face, or on any other face for that matter.

"I had a nightmare".

"And I envied you".

Quite unexpectedly, walking by the Coed Elementary School of Spilia, she heard the children make a collective invocation for the salvation of "Miss Avgi".

"And spare her, Lord, from any danger, disease or need".

She paused; the exhortation was repeated. Then they prayed, collectively again, for grandpa Matthew and an old lady she didn't know. A boy was reciting the names, with the chorus repeating the spell: "Because, God, you are great, benign and benevolent".

Frustrated, she was ready to walk on, but the Principal caught up with her; he had noticed her and rushed to say hello. He asked if he could walk with her, having a free hour as he did.

"Yes, of course you may".

They walked in silence for a while. Then she stopped brusquely, turned and snapped at him:

"I heard the prayer; your idea?"

"Not at all! Far from it".

And he explained how, according to a recent decision by the School Goodwill Committee, part of the Religious Affairs class was devoted to one or more members of the community "in need of aid from above" – as verbalized by the Committee Chairman, Father Stavros.

"Why Avgi?"

"The children insisted", he said in his defence. "There is, you see, a special subcommittee chaired by the priest's grandson. It's their decision to make. They presume that, for their beloved teacher to disappear out of the blue, something serious must have happened. You know how they are, children. Always confusing serious with bad".

"And you? Do you agree?"

"Not exactly. However, it's not only that. The fact is, I myself had noticed a change in Avgi. She was so agitated and nervous; in fact, we had gotten word she had been seen in tears... twice; at her house and in the schoolyard, during the break. At some point she regained her composure, went back to her usual pleasant, humorous self. I should also add that, according to Miss Agapiou, one of her young pupils, three or four times of late she was seen during an interval between classes sitting still on the stairs, like a statue, staring into the void. The girl's report was corroborated by the school's cleaning lady. It's a combination of things…"

"And does that provide a reason for her to be pitied by the entire village?"

"This is not precisely the case, dear Maria. What I've just mentioned has taken on new meaning and significance after her disappearance. Also, let's not forget how things are in our villages. You'll see for yourself in time, though not from experience, I hope".

Maria Akritas did not reply; she decided that the inquisition had come to an end, though it brought nothing of essence to the surface; nor was there any reason for her to carry on this idiocy, seeing that the deeper she poked, the more furious she became, exacerbating her interlocutor's awkwardness. After all, a prayer, albeit useless, can do no harm. And she changed the subject; she said that Joseph and she had decided to invite some friends over for dinner on Saturday night and it would give them great pleasure if he could make it.

"It'll be you, Father Stavros and… the Archangielsks, hopefully. All three of them!"

He accepted with distinct pleasure.

"And, thankfully, your invitation comes six whole days ahead", he said, brimming with a smile. "Not that my schedule's so busy that I'd have to keep the night free. It's just that… I'll have something lovely to look forward to for six whole days!"

As they kept on walking along the alleys of the village, they talked of the two conservators and their guest. Mr Demetriades had visited them again the day before. Yes, at the Chapel, with his six-graders; and, on the same night, on the upper floor, with the priest.

"They're planning on issuing a scientific announcement regarding the wall-painting, on the request of the Cyprus Archaeological Museum and UNESCO. I believe that, over the past weeks, they had worked closely with your friend, Miss Avgi in order to draft it. Tell me, did Joseph give you my message for noon?"

"Yes, he did. I'll join you".

They walked on, in silence again. Then she asked him:

"Is the young man an icon painter too or just a painter?"

"Michael? No, he's a musician; a very talented one no less! I must say, I do know a few things about music, from Chatzidakis to Bach, Byzantine music too! But what I heard him play last night was… unprecedented. And he only used a guitar. Just six strings! It was like the Aegean sun, frolicking with the waves and celestial bodies. Indescribable, akin to… no, it can only be defined as something inconceivable and indescribable. When we left, I was so enchanted, so deeply immersed in a daze, dreamy inebriation – probably because of that incredible wine of theirs, I'm sure – that I went about breaking down my thoughts and reactions for Father Stavros; I should've known better! He threatened to excommunicate me if I didn't keep my peace… What can I say, I'm mesmerized!"

"What he played, did he compose it himself?"

"I should think so! He composed and performed it of course!" He laughed. "I actually asked him the same thing! He looked at me in silence, as if he hadn't heard me. Hanna replied, a bit later, as she served wine. 'It's no one's', she told me. 'But someone must have composed it'. – 'Precisely! And someone else had replicated it!' – 'It's reversal on a different level', Piotr had joined in. I think this is what they meant, but they never said. Or maybe not. Anyway! The main thing, my dear Maria, is that we have important people in our village!" Demetriades exclaimed. "Them! You! Joseph!"

"Now you're definitely up for excommunication".

"And my gifted colleague, Miss Avgi!"

The thought of her wiped the smile off his face.

"I met them too, yesterday afternoon, by chance. They said they wanted to see me, to talk about something".

"There you go, you can do it at noon".

"I hope I can make it, with so much snow".

"I'm sure that if I can do it... But it's true, the weather this year! Did you know this is the heaviest snowfall since 1890?"

He was interrupted by the bell resounding from the other end of the street. He paused, looked into the void absentmindedly. Then, as if in a soliloquy, pursued the thread of a previous thought:

"Indeed, we do have important people in the village! Only our priest seems unable to come to terms with it. Perhaps because I don't include him. That man is a sinner, Lord forgive me! Do you know what he said to me the other day? You won't believe it. He doesn't think highly of the two 'Jewish Archangels'. Even though they live and work in the Lord's House six days a week, they never attend his mass".

"Come to think of it, I'm not sure I should be accompanying you. You did say they needed to talk to you".

"What would they say to me that they can't say in front of you?"

"Who knows the will of the Archangielsks?" Demetriades joked, laughing on his own.

Crossing the yard of the house, they walked out onto the street, or what was left of it after the orgiastic snowfall. The dog followed suit.

. . . .

"What about Joseph? Didn't he want to come with you?"

"He's gone to the city".

. . . .

"This is the cemetery, right?"

"Yes, we'll turn right from here".

. . . .

As they walked past the low wall that was adorned with the remains of withered bindweed, she decided to take a look inside, randomly counting the crosses. Everything was covered in snow. Of the crosses, only a few marble or wooden arms came into view, together with pots of wilted flowers. Her courage ran out with the first glance she threw at the tombs and, with a brusque gesture, she clutched at her escort's arm.

"What's the matter?" Demetriades asked, alarmingly. "Are you dizzy?"

"I'm cold".

"It's only natural! Do you know how much the temperature has dropped from one day to the next? By twenty degrees! First time in recent years. Imagine how I must feel, when I'm usually cold in mid-summer!"

She leant and picked up a shrub to carve into the sleet that lay ahead.

"Did you ever wonder why there is... why there needs to be so much desolation in the world? Why do we have to pay so dearly for the little we get?"

"I didn't know you were interested in philosophy".

"If what I just said is philosophy, then everyone who's like me is a philosopher. In fact, we're better than those sitting neatly behind their offices, scribbling away, instead of wracking their brain to find solutions".

"But, are there any solutions?"

"If they could at least try... I mean, how much do we ask? You can always make do with less".

....

"Euthanasia, for instance!"

....

"You remind me of Avgi. Of late she too talked in riddles. It's as if you're repeating..."

"Does this surprise you? You should have known that, if you really look into it, this world lacks originality".

....

"Then?"

....

"What's the point? When death is a sine qua non, then every fight is in vain, dear Kyros!"

....

"When?"

....

"Always. But you do know that just as I do. Joseph does too. We all know and possess it. But we won't give it over. Because we are petty. There is nothing we guard the most than what we know the other needs, what we know will make him happy; and there's nothing we put to more waste…"

"I think you're exaggerating a bit".

"Do you now?"

. . . .

She threw away the branch she had used for a while as a rod. The dog secured it in its mouth before letting it fall to the ground.

"Take it home as a token of remembrance", she ordered it. The dog looked at her, wagged its tail and ran in the direction of the village. Now, amidst the trees, the roof of the chapel emerged. "Indeed! It's much closer from here".

. . . .

"There's always a shortcut".

. . . .

"There certainly is!"

"As a rule we opt for the most difficult road".

"God forbid we chose otherwise".

"How boring our life would be".

"Would it?"

. . . .

"You really are frigid".

In spite of their strategy, to never and for no reason interrupt their work — except for a cup of wine and fruit at ten in the morning, at noon for lunch and then at five once the day's work was done — this time the Archangielsks broke their own rule. No sooner had they seen them than with a sprightliness that was amazing for their age, they climbed down the scaffold and warmly shook the hands of Maria and her escort.

"We are glad you came", they both said at the same time. "You're exactly as he described you", Hanna's voice stood out as she carried on.

"And how did you describe me?" Maria asked Michael, somewhat numbed by the reception they were offered. He was coming out of the Holy Bema through the Beautiful Gate.

He didn't respond.

Mr Archangielsk cupped her cold palm with his, large and warm, and said on his behalf:

"Just as you had described Avgi to him!"

Her concealed angst was defused with a feeling of self-confidence. How naïve, she thought. Could a mere compliment reverse her mood so swiftly? It had, of course. But to what avail?

"Thank you", she said, as she observed Michael approaching in silence, looking into her eyes.

His gaze embarrassed her. To avoid it, she turned hers away. The illustration on the wall gave her the escape she was looking for.

"So… these are the wall-paintings you have re…restored, aren't they?"

"It's not a restoration", Hanna Archangielsk politely corrected her. "It's a revelation".

"A recovery", Piotr either added or amended.

"How do you work exactly?" Maria asked. "Until recently, last year to be exact, this chapel had…"

"…milky walls", Hanna offered. "The villagers' piety had it whitewashed year after year on the feast day of the Three Holy Youths! Sometimes even more frequently, twice, thrice per year. For us to reach the fresco, the colour, we unveil every thin surface of lime deposited with each whitewash; ninety in all, added over a span of sixty years. We remove them, one after the other. Then we start clearing the representations and bringing out the colours, one by one, using special brushes and chemicals. Every section and colour requires the same or even more meticulous care and technique as the ones first applied by the painter; otherwise, there's a risk of distorting or destroying them".

"Hanna! Hanna!" Piotr comically despaired. "Time and again I have asked you not to betray our few secrets! How are we to survive if we ourselves unveil the mystery shrouding our craft?"

Smiling, Hanna took off her glasses and rubbed her eyes.

"You do not need these secrets to survive", Demetriades spoke for the first time since they arrived, pointing to the wall-paintings. "Quite the opposite, really".

"It's strange!" Maria whispered, approaching the scaffold; larger parts of the wall-painting emerged from within the joints.

Piotr swiftly went up the scaffold.

"I'll shed light", Michael said.

He grabbed hold of a portable spotlight from the corner, put it in place and plugged it into a set of batteries. Light washed over the image. Around it, a pure white wall carrying ninety layers of lime; and two to three fingers below, within a circular surface with a radius of approximately two meters, the colours ignited.

"The theme of the composition is evidently the Nativity", Piotr explained, wearing the glasses his wife had taken off a moment ago. "You see", he went on, "we share the same degree of far-sightedness". And he smiled at the paradox. "For the time being, we have revealed this head here with the four-ray circle; as far as we know, it is unique to the entire Byzantine icon-painting style. Look carefully; doesn't it remind you of someone you know? Someone you would have liked to know better? Someone giving you hope and a way out? Do not attempt to name him right away. It's he that Ms Akritas thought of. And he that Mr Demetriades thought of too, that all of us thought of on our own".

"...Christ", Maria spontaneously muttered.

"Yes! For the reason I have pointed out", Piotr ascertained and climbed down the scaffold.

"It couldn't have been otherwise", Hanna smiled.

"What about the other figures, around the image?"

"The shepherd herding the sins of the world! The horned head of the lamb with the enraged eyes! This is what it depicts, I believe. Or the pack of maladies, each malady a passion, a deathly pain of mind. But this we shall see as we carry on. As for the other figure, that one there, only partially discerned, it's still incomplete. I presume it's a woman, suffering; extending her hand. Once freed from lime she'll perhaps reveal what despair directs and guides her hand. The other figures haven't been exposed yet, only partially. A woman's knee, a man's arm, perhaps the magi or other shepherds. But there's something else that's amazing; the fresco technique! And the choice of figures! They are utterly contemporary. They're more contemporary today than at the time they were historicized by the painter. Just compare them to any other wall-painting of the 11th century. Nowhere is the technique or faces as modern as they are ancient at the same time".

"Perhaps they are of the future also", Hanna added, gently removing the glasses from him. "I'd better take those from you; go on like that and you'll bore our friends".

"Far from it".

"Tell me, my dears", Piotr exclaimed in feigned despair, "was Perseus right or wrong in stealing the witches' only eye, their only tooth and ear?"

They all laughed and the spotlight went out. The colours faded, penumbra and shadows returned to the church.

"Your impressions?" Piotr Archangielsk asked Maria Akritas.

"Excellent!" she vaguely replied, unable to define the emotions the wall-painting had awakened within her.

"Then, I will dare talk to you of that other matter; you do recall, I had mentioned something on the street, the other day".

"Well, Mikael, Mr Demetriades and myself are going outside in the lovely snow; you can talk as you please", Hanna said and the three of them went outside, walking arm-in-arm.

Piotr led Maria to the only pew in the chapel. He sat opposite her on a stool of giant fennel. Behind him, in a candelabrum, the flame of a candle flickered, the glare blurring her vision.

"Hanna and I are writing an essay on the wall-painting of the Three Holy Youths", he got straight to the point. "We believe that your contribution would be valuable".

"But…" Maria offered coyly, disappointed after realizing what they required of her.

"I know what you're going to say; that the essay is premature seeing that our work here has not been completed yet. I could counter that by suggesting that the head alone is worth not just one book but a whole series".

"That's not what I meant", Maria said. "I'm afraid I'm not the best choice. I lack the terminology, I don't have any writing skill or talent and, above all, I'm afraid this particular topic does not interest me enough to make me put everything else aside".

"Allow me once more to doubt that, precisely for the reasons you have cited. Though it may seem strange to you, we actually think of them as advantages. You will be the first inexpert and perceptive judge of the ideas we are to set forth. Miss Avgi had similar reservations but I assure you once we started, she realized they were utterly ungrounded".

"I suggest you wait for her. At some point, soon we hope, she'll come back. It's best you carry on with her. Avgi is really good at such things".

"When she returns, we'll work together; the four of us". He stopped for a moment to regroup, then added: "There's something else I'd like to clear before we begin; the matter of your fee. Because our finances do not allow the luxury of a secretary, you will be granted one quarter of the book's intellectual property rights. That is, if the project is ever completed and the book published".

"Oh, it's not a question of remuneration. If..."

"You must allow us to insist on that. Our will and decision is for our cooperation to be placed on a professional basis; which will give us the right to claim your undistracted attention. Miss Avgi had worked with us under the same conditions".

"I understand, but I assure you, that's the last thing that... it's neither the money nor the time required! There are other reasons, utterly private ones, that do not allow me to engage in such a far-reaching project".

"Then", Piotr said, "I will insist no further; I only wish that the reasons that will deprive us of the joy of working with you are indeed pleasant ones. If this is the case, then no one has the right to impose on you a project that will require the maximum of your attention, toil and, I will not deny it, several sacrifices. At any rate, my dear Maria, I personally recommend that you reconsider our proposition; the most effective manner for someone to deal with a problem is through committed work".

"Do you believe in work therapy?"

"I believe in contributing".

A long pause followed. Then, Piotr Archangielsk riveted his bright eyes on her.

"Well? Will you reflect upon it? Give it some thought and get back to us".

"Very well", Maria said and stood up.

"One last question", she quickly added. "Why did you choose me specifically? I mean, even in a village like Spilia you are bound to find people that are much more appropriate and willing than me. Mr Demetriades, for instance. Or... Mr Akritas!"

"You have had the best recommendations".

"By whom?"

"By Mikael. And Miss Avgi. You know, we've known you for a while now, since the first day we met your friend and since you met Mikael".

"Will you allow me one more question?"

"Certainly".

"How long do you think it will take you to write this... essay?"

"As much time needed for our own work! Nine months. But I do warn you; if you acquiesce, then for this entire period, perhaps a bit longer too, you will belong to us in body and soul; we won't allow any infidelities".

"Well, these things are not always up to us".

"Entirely up to us", Piotr said in the same calm tone.

And even though nothing in his voice or expression suggested he meant to emphasize the meaning of his words, Maria felt a shiver down her spine and a... If she took on the task, if she said yes, perhaps her angst would... perhaps the interval would become more...

Yet, she didn't rush to say the 'yes' she now felt was her only escape. She chose to change the subject and told him about dinner on Saturday and how happy they would be to have them, all three of them!

"Then we'll be there", Piotr responded.

"This Saturday, eight o' clock".

Faces flushed, Hanna Archangielsk, Mr Demetriades and Michael returned from hiking, all three of them a supplement and a consequence of the ensuing pause.

"Did you two talk?" Hanna asked her husband, both her keenness and gaze revealing awareness of the effort he had had to make.

"Yes. Maria promised to consider our proposition", he replied.

"But of course".

And she looked Maria in the eyes; in hers, the young woman saw vivid encouragement and maybe, or this is how she chose to interpret it, a promise.

"Maria and Joseph, the Akritases, are inviting us for dinner at their house this Saturday", Piotr Archangielsk announced. "I do believe we can make it".

Before answering, Hanna looked at the youth inquisitively.

"Mikael?"

"We'll go", he positively responded.

Upon the expression of the Archangielsks, Maria saw no trace of surprise or discontent for the youth's undisputable, categorical tone. What she discerned on their faces as they watched him moving away until he disappeared behind the Beautiful Gate, was love and acceptance.

"This gives me great joy, gives us great joy…" Maria rephrased. "We'll be waiting for you".

No one replied.

"Well, Maria? I think it's time for us to go…" Mr Demetriades said. "We've kept the…" he had trouble finding the right word. "We've kept Mr and Ms Archangielsk and Michael from their work long enough".

"On the contrary", Piotr replied. "We never stopped working, neither Hanna nor I".

"During our walk in the snowy forest, he talked of Patmos in such simple yet lucid words; never before had I heard anyone praise his homeland so eloquently; and in fact, praise the entire world… I've never been there, but I seem to miss it, perhaps because I love the sea, dream of it. Travels too… and atonement in the Sacred Grotto!"

. . . .

"Riveted; without any special capacities".

. . . .

"Children of the tragic Thyestes".

. . . .

"Crucified; with no expectation of a resurrection".

. . . .

"Our only escape has ended up being sleep".

. . . .

"What for others is a given even before they begin, for us remain inapproachable targets, a utopia".

. . . .

"I would like to erase and erase, start from the beginning".

. . . .

"I've never felt as trapped, riveted to what is unworthy of reference. And to think there are people who've known the world since their early twenties and can speak seven languages fluently. And we, the unrepentant ones, who have wasted our life trying to turn the innocent children we've been entrusted with into proper citizens of Spilia and Kourdali... Feeding them with manure and carcass... Why should God take pity on us, why absolve us?"

. . . .

"He suggested I help them; in Avgi's place. No, I'll probably say no. I'm the last person that could, the last who's interested in wall-paintings and book writing. I've read nothing but cheap romances and fashion magazines, and even those during the interval between my worldly activities, cinema and TV".

"And now... It seems that nothing comes without reason".

"I really liked the word "pack" they used. It fits so well with everything we've seen, everything we've been going through..."

"Did you notice what they called him? Mikael! Like the Archangel, protector of the poor and weak".

. . . .

"Yes, I am aware of the advantages and the other issues that may arise. I'll think about it and decide for myself".

. . . .

"It's always appealing to us, believing that for everything, no matter how big or small, it is we who decide, we who always have the last word".

The following day, grandpa Matthew died. It took a great effort to convince Father Stavros to allow the son and grandchildren of the deceased to execute his last will: entwine the worry beads between his rigid fingers.

"Won't he have anything else to do up there, the old man? For God's sake, what would he want with the worry beads?"

"Give it a rest", the Sergeant intervened. "With his hearing, I reckon it'll take him ages to learn to play the lyre. How will he kill time, poor man?"

The earth underneath the snow had become rock solid; the entire family had spent the entire morning working in shifts with a jackhammer and a shovel in order to dig the grave.

Instead of mud or snow, Maria Akritas threw a handful of white roses on grandpa's face.

Kyros Demetriades and Father Stavros were the first to arrive;

the latter carried two demijohns: commandaria and raki of his own production. Demetriades brought a pile of books: "Art and Music in the Byzantium", "Asinou", "Learn without tears: Written Discourse".

Joseph Akritas welcomed them at the door; he took their presents, thanked them and led them to the living room, where the fireplace took centre stage. Father Stavros apologized on behalf of his *presbytera*; she was confined to bed with asthma and, though she would have loved to come, she couldn't make it.

The host offered to serve drinks, but his two guests opted to wait "for the others" and sat comfortably. Joseph took his whiskey from the travertine slab on the fireplace and sat next to Demetriades, on the black humble stool that Maria had dressed in sheepskin for the occasion.

"What's new?" the priest asked. "It's been days since we last saw you at the coffee-shop".

"Yes. I was rather indisposed".

"Nothing serious, I hope", Demetriades said.

Akritas waved no and thanked him with a detached, distracted smile.

"Well, driving back and forth to Nicosia and elsewhere doesn't help either..." Father Stavros offered. "I imagine you're on the move for Avgi..."

Akritas did not react. But Father Stavros never took silence for an answer. After all, in his own words, he always made sure he had "an ace up his sleeve". So he went on:

"Say, have there been any developments with your other case? Have the heads of the Agency convinced you yet?"

Akritas gave him a vague look, unwilling to reply.

"I meant about your reportage. Word has it they're adamant about broadcasting it one way or another".

"And where might I ask did you learn that, Father?" Demetriades inquired in surprise and admiration.

"Completely by chance! From a journalist friend. I ran into him in Troodos", replied the man of cloth.

Demetriades wasn't buying it; it was common knowledge that chance was completely foreign to the character of his friend, Father Stavros Alexandrinos.

"It is a fact, my dear Joseph, that this time you deprived us of the... experience of reading your reports", said the Principal of the Elementary School. "I don't mean to flatter you but your texts and films, at least those I have seen... are amongst the few things that causes one embarrassment over his human capacity. There's no reason to hide it, in fact I often remark how proud I am to know you and share a glass of *zivania* with you from time to time".

Father Stavros nodded in agreement.

"Indeed though... aren't you going to have it published?" Demetriades asked again, wary over his persistence. "In the newspaper the other day, I don't remember which one, I read that on this particular mission you had done an amazing job! Not that your previous contributions fell short, not at all! I have to say, I do look forward to reading it".

"These things must definitely be read!" Father Stavros agreed. "If there's something we must often read it's our own bestialities".

"Haven't you completed your... could I call it an illustrated story?" Demetriades asked with guilty perseverance.

"I did complete it", Akritas snapped, annoyed. He smiled to assuage the impression he gave with his crude, coarse tone. Then he added: "But I do not intend to have it published".

"That's a shame! Why?" the priest resumed the inquisition.

"Personal reasons".

"No one's pressuring you, dear Joseph", Father Stavros said in camouflaged discontent.

"I know that", Akritas replied, then: "I think it's time for a drink".

"Yes, I would gladly have something; cognac or whiskey", the priest offered in the same, somewhat disgruntled tone.

"What about you?"

"Something light, thank you", Demetriades answered.

Maria Akritas walked into the room. The two guests immediately stood up and said hello, the priest by nodding his bald head, the teacher by slightly bowing. The hostess apologized for being late, inquired after the *papadia* and the school, and asked them to take their seats. She was wearing a black gown, fine lace around the hem and sleeves, its only adornment an old smoked-silver coin below the closed collar. Her hair, loose, fell shiny and rich to the small of her back. On her left temple, a second coin, identical to the other, held it pinned behind the ear. A bride in mourning.

In spite of themselves, the two men looked at her with genuine admiration; never, in the past five years they had known her, had they suspected she was so feminine, so inaccessibly beautiful! Her skin had a translucent quality that was accentuated by the torrent of her hair; she always wore it back, using a large hairpin shaped after a butterfly. Her loose black dress, the fire that crackled and spat sparks, the highlights cast on her face, her cheeks, her hair, by the rustic candelabra-turned-chandelier crafted by the imaginative, inventive Avgi.

"What will you have?" Akritas asked her, untouched by and indifferent to the disruption caused by his wife's entrance.

"Nothing, Joseph, thank you".

"But you must have something with us", Demetriades said. How else are we going to drink to… to you?" he struggled to finish his sentence.

Maria offered him a friendly smile.

"Alright then, some juice please".

"You can't drink juice to the glory of God", the priest protested.

"My goodness!" Demetriades said. "When you're paying compliments, no one can compete with you!"

"Simply because I'm not doing what you are suggesting. I only speak the truth".

Drinks were distributed amidst the silence followed by Father Stavros' remark.

"To our health", Akritas made an unemotional toast.

"Good to be here", the guests replied according to the traditional order. And they clinked their glasses together forming an X, Demetriades with Joseph and the priest with the hostess. Then, the two guests among themselves.

Akritas had no other option than to clink, or barely touch, his glass with hers. The crystal resonated.

"To Avgi's return", Father Stavros made a wish.

"To the return of the dear colleague and friend", Demetriades repeated.

"Another round?" Maria offered as soon as they emptied their glasses.

"In a bit, thank you", Demetriades replied.

"Yes for me", said Father Stavros. "We are not done with toasting".

"It appears we are a bit early", Demetriades rushed to cut him in and changed the subject lest the silent Akritas took offence.

"Why are we early?" the priest protested.

"From what I've heard, the Archangielsks are always punctual; they can't be late, therefore we barged in early".

"Why? What time is it?" Father Stavros asked.

"Five to eight", Demetriades consulted the round pocket watch he kept in his black vest. "Yes, I do remember now... We said eight, not seven thirty". And, in an apologetic tone, he turned to the priest: "See? I told you so. I was certain. We do beg your pardon!"

"Not at all", Maria replied. "Your company is always pleasant".

"You are too kind", Demetriades reciprocated the compliment.

"Thank you", said the hostess and immediately added: "Do excuse us for keeping to ourselves!"

"Please, dear Maria! We know this is what you seek in the village. Especially Joseph, tired as he must be from a journey of several months".

"And that's why we didn't bother you earlier", Father Stavros added. "But now that you're encouraging us..."

"Our friends never bother us", Maria said.

"It's an honour", Demetriades smiled. "You'd better not repeat it because we're bound to....take advantage of it! Of course, there's this unfortunate incident with Avgi, her disappearance I mean; had us all upset. Today I received an official notice; they're sending us a substitute".

Maria rekindled the fire. Soft exchanges and steps were heard from outside.

They stood by the rail; it creaked. They walked up the driveway that had been meticulously cleared of the snow, stopped at the front door. Before they knocked, Maria was there. Behind her, at a distance of reluctance, Joseph Akritas.

The pendulum clock in the hall sounded eight.

"Good evening! There you are! Do come in!"

Hanna brought a cake of her home country, made of nuts, cream and ground almonds. She placed it on the coffee table in the hall. Piotr gave the hostess a seal-stone he had found while excavating a temple in Jerusalem; it was a copper coin with an embossed figure on one side, that of a youth emptying water from a ewer. A two thousand year-old date was engraved on the reverse side.

"I hope you like it", he said.

"It's lovely", Maria exclaimed on impulse. "And astrologically poignant, reminding us that we've entered the sign and age of the Aquarius, the Water Bearer". Then she protested: "There was no need for gifts".

"They're *antidora*, return gifts, with our thanks", Hanna answered on behalf of both.

They took off their coats. Joseph took them and hung them on the portmanteau, where a while ago he had placed the package of books and the two demijohns.

"Mr Demetriades brought the books for you. This is from Father Stavros", he informed her.

"For *us*", she softly corrected him and took a quick look at the books; she was always amazed by the manner in which Demetriades' mind worked: his inspired methodicalness and unusual, for someone who'd spent half his life in small villages, tact.

She placed the books upside-down to hide their titles and searched for Michael's eyes, something she'd been wanting to do for some time now.

"Well?" she asked him when the others walked into the living room.

"I'll play for you", he told her and reciprocated her gaze.

She couldn't bear that look that was both piercing and tender. She lowered her eyes. She wanted to be utterly beautiful, to keep herself from panicking in front of this youthful, androgynous face; or utterly healthy in order to hope.

They walked into the living room as the others were exchanging handshakes. Michael greeted them with a friendly nod of the head. They all sat comfortably; Hanna next to Demetriades, Piotr on a rustic armchair and Michael on the woven woollen rug next to Maria.

"What would you like to drink?" Akritas asked.

"Wine for me, local if you have", Piotr kindly ordered.

"By all means! Father Stavros has made sure of that, bringing us a whole demijohn! And another of local raki, *zivania!*"

"We thank you all for your gifts!" Maria availed herself of the opportunity. "For presents like these I could be hosting a party every Saturday!"

"Well, I assure you, you will be the first to have a change of heart..." Demetriades said.

"And you? What will you have?" Akritas asked Hanna Archangielsk.

"I'll have some wine too".

Maria turned to Michael with a smile:

"And you?"

"Fruit juice", he replied.

"Orange? Grape?"

"Whatever".

Maria stepped out of the room; Michael's gaze persistently followed her.

"How fares your work? Any new surprises?" Demetriades asked.

"None! It appears we are quite old; from now on, nothing can surprise us", Piotr replied.

Maria offered drinks to the three guests, as Joseph served another round for the first two. After the typical toasting, that the three avoided with a smile or an imperceptible raising of glasses, and after they all took a first sip, Demetriades was the first to speak:

"Allow me to make a wish to the fruition of your project! For you, it may well be routine, as you say, but for us, and for the village of Spilia, it's the biggest thing that has happened for years! Am I right, Father?"

And he gulped down his drink.

"We never said our work was routine", Piotr politely corrected him.

"We only said that nothing could surprise us!" Hanna joined in.

"I often wonder what the benefit is in continuing to embellish vanity!" Akritas ironically observed.

"What do you mean exactly?" Father Stavros interjected. "Because if you mean what I think you do, then you are right!"

Maria looked annoyed and intensely puzzled over her husband's unexpected remark. Though in essence she thought it was quite right, in this particular case, and given the nature of the gathering, she found it untimely and irrelevant.

"I am talking about the vanity of the human effort", Akritas went on in the same tone. "Both for those who do surprise and those who don't. I know this is a simplification but the central essence is still there; concomitant to our orbit".

"And what orbit is that? I do not follow", Demetriades asked with a smidgen of guilt over the stiffness of his mind.

"The one and only; from darkness to grief and from grief to darkness".

"I can't follow either", Father Stavros revised what he had said earlier. "I had assumed…"

"Me too, precisely… Of course, personally, I have no reason to disagree; though for many there are ways of escape. Art, eros, children and, often, ignorance. We all find something. For me, for instance, it's this night. I don't know what it means to the others, but to me this night is a pleasant pause, a long pause, a welcome break of life. I imagine the same goes for our dear priest. It began with this invitation and it will last until the next one". Then, smiling, he added: "I wonder what Mr Archangielsk has to say about all this".

"I'm listening".

"More wine?" the hostess offered, naively hoping that by refreshing the drinks she would steer the conversation back to less treacherous paths. And she stood up to underline her will.

"Ms Archangielsk?"

"Thank you, later".

She turned to the youth:

"You haven't touched your juice. Do you prefer something else?"

"I feel complete... Therefore, please, forget about me".

"How could I?" Maria asked in surprise. And, catching herself acting spontaneously, almost childishly, for the first time in months, she blushed. "Time to have a bite then", she added as cheerfully. "It's almost eight thirty. And I'm hungry".

"Likewise!" the priest concurred.

Somewhat reassured by her small victory, Maria asked Joseph to help her. They pulled aside the folding doors that separated the living room from the dining hall, to reveal the table, set for some time now: lamb on a skewer, grilled fish, turkey with pilaf filling, sausages, village salad, feta cheese, yogurt, peas, halloumi, minced meat burek and almond "lady fingers" for dessert.

"We opted for local cuisine", explained Maria.

"Marvellous! Marvellous!" Father Stavros enthusiastically exclaimed.

They each took a plate; the guests stood in a queue by the table. The priest served himself first, by right of order. Then, Hanna Archangielsk; Piotr Archangielsk; Kyros Demetriades; Michael. And last, the hosts.

The most impressive plate was crafted by Father Stavros; it was a pyramid of generous helpings of everything, enmeshed between three slices of bread at the bottom and three at the top. Demetriades was frugal; he chose the lighter options: fish, peas, a piece of lamb, fatless, and strained yoghurt. The Archangielsks limited their servings to pilaf, village salad and greens. Michael only had fruit. Aware of the three guests' preferences, Maria didn't pressure them to taste her dishes, nor did she make any suggestions. Only Father Stavros cast a furtive glance at them, a flash of irony in his eyes, whilst chewing on the fatty lamb with pronounced pleasure.

"Is it true you've never tasted meat?" he finally asked, unable to resist the temptation, and indeed so impulsively that he had no time to put it more discreetly.

"Yes, we are vegetarians", Hanna replied with a smile.

"By conviction or tradition?" the priest resumed.

"By love", Piotr answered.

After a brief, awkward pause, Father Stavros regrouped and spoke again:

"What you say I understand and respect. Nevertheless, as a man of the cloth, I am curious to see whether you consider meat-eating a sin".

"It is and it isn't", Michael replied on behalf of the three guests.

"The fact that you have excluded meat from your diet means, I presume, that you consider it a sin", the priest carried on the amical inquisition.

"No, given our belief that sins, as most people understand them, do not exist", replied the youth. "Just as there are no virtues that may remain universally acknowledged through time".

"Is that what you think?" the priest asked, now annoyed and more contentious. He went on, losing the polite tone: "And if in your opinion there are neither sins nor virtues, then what would you say lurks upon the path we have been treading since our birth?"

"Many and great things! First of all, the incessant evolution of targets, perceptions and beliefs".

"Hence the eternal changes, since the first hour of human life on earth", Hanna added, "changes sometimes transpiring over millennia or centuries. In our time they take place within decades, and they are of the same age as any landmark evolution".

"To philosophize and theorize..." the priest sneered.

"What about you, dear Michael? What's your take on this particular matter?" Demetriades interjected his question between the others' dialogue, whilst casting a beseeching look at the priest, with a hidden nod to take the sting out of the conversation. "Surely, a youth in his twenties must ponder the fight between good and evil! After all, I can't accept that a young man can reach the neutrality of the vegetative state, that of the late grandpa Matthew. Can he?"

"That's a good question, Kyros. What do you say, son? Can you?" the priest spoke again.

"I do try, indeed train myself, to be free of both states".

"I'm afraid that's not what I asked, dear Michael. What I want to know is, based on your personal theory, between good and evil, which one would you choose?" Demetriades resumed.

"Whichever is compatible with what expresses my free will and judgement on the day of the choice; the eumorphic today, tomorrow the dysmorphic, the amorphous the day after tomorrow. In other words, everything that comprises our life, the world around and within us".

"That's a very odd and elastic freedom you describe!" the priest snickered.

"And is there no risk of, inadvertently of course, leading yourself to extremities? To serious or even fatal errors?" Demetriades raised the level of controversy once more.

"No. Because I have love", the youth began, without any attempt at rhetoric or emphasis.

"So there is at least one requirement! That's something!" Father Stavros interrupted him to taunt.

"Love is not only a requirement; it's a guarantee, a conquest. The greatest there is! It abolishes and revokes, averts and permits", Michael peacefully concluded his answer.

There was another long pause. Maria broke it.

"How do we achieve this? Can anyone free themselves like that, just like you say? Well…"

"They can, Maria, we can! If we live our lives on the point of balance, consciously; if we prudently engage with the opposites, liberated from prejudice and self-restrictions; if and when we achieve this, then we start being free of any kind of slavery, we act independent of laws and consequences, we live! We live blissfully!"

"That's a very hoity-toity way of looking at things!" the priest said to himself. And, turning to the youth, "You are far too young to speak this way, lad", he added, with a calmness afforded by the conviction he was dealing with a halfwit.

"And we're far too old to judge an age-old youth", Piotr Archangielsk offered.

"What does that mean? How do you…" Demetriades asked, feeling words and senses slipping away from him, adding to his excitement.

There was no reply, as if the question had never been posed.

"This is the age of youth", Hanna spoke after the pause. "We are living in the time of the reversal of ages, just as we had lived the reversal of values and a thousand other treasured valuables".

Joseph, long drawn in by the dialogue, joined in, mesmerized:

"Yes, the lady is right, we do live in times of reversals. Not in the time of youth; the time of reversing anything that's beautiful and alive and youthful and healthy and free; the time portending not life and love or the utopic bliss that was mentioned a moment ago, but their complete and utter erasure!"

Maria looked at him, curious and moved; what he said about life and their age and Michael too may not be true, or true the way she would have wanted it to be, but alas; it was true and timely as far as she was concerned, it actually *was* her! And it definitely was him!

Demetriades and Father Stavros were relieved over his siding with them in the discordance, or so they construed his intervention.

"Life cannot be erased, dear Joseph; by no means", Piotr Archangielsk calmly opposed him.

"And if, at times it runs the risk of extinction, this does not happen on account of God, Joseph", Father Stavros put his flow of thoughts into words. "It happens on account of us".

"On account of Him who, after your own teachings, Father, has made us in His image and likeness", Akritas resumed. "Perishable! So what's the point of so much pain and depravity? Wasn't the unavoidable death bad enough? What's the point of suffering Job's afflictions? So that we may learn through our sores? Or that He may be glorified with our purported resurrection, when we need nothing but a reasonable extension of peaceful life, if nowhere else, then here, in Spilia and Kourdali!"

Maria looked at Michael and the Archangielsks, expecting that one of them would reply, would attempt to somehow widen the terrible restraints that Akritas imposed on the discussion. But none of them spoke; nor did she notice any reaction in their gaze. They remained impartial and inscrutable, as always.

"I do not agree with what you said, dear Joseph; not at all!" the priest spoke. "Let's not charge our faults and imperfections to God".

"Nothing of the sort", Akritas replied even more calmly. "It is cowardly to assign responsibilities to the inexistent, the primordial object of our vanity!"

"The void! The inexistent! And us in between", Demetriades dared step into the vortex. "We, who live and love, and suffer and hope. How is this possible?"

"We, the zero squared", Akritas resumed forthrightly.

Suddenly he stopped, then, breaking a sweat, he got up and rushed to the bathroom.

"It's best to change the subject", a perturbed Demetriades muttered, as Joseph's prolonged coughing and fierce vomiting were heard through the bathroom.

For a few minutes, silence fell inside the room. There was nothing but the crackling of burning wood and, from outside on the street, the barking of the dog.

Without any prearrangement between him and Michael, Piotr walked to the hall and returned with the guitar. He removed its cloth case and gave it to the youth.

"Thank you", he said, as he took it.

"At last, a fine idea!" the priest applauded the move.

"Let's wait for Joseph", Demetriades suggested. "The music might... might appease all of us. What do you say, Father?"

"Indeed", the priest concurred. And, turning to Michael: "Can you play any island tunes, child?"

Maria left the room; she found Joseph bent over the sink, washing his face and hands. With a towel she wiped his damp face, eyes and mouth, still soiled with remnants of vomit.

"You're right", she whispered to him. "I wish you weren't".

He looked at her.

"I'm sorry you understand…"

"We have to go back in, Joseph".

"Why do we have to, Maria?"

They were mesmerized by the music. The guest had begun to improvise with the strings.

Joseph followed Maria.

The music, plain, without a solid theme or melodic cohesion; uncontracted cells of matter ascending fervently, igniting like fireworks, then fading; a river of shooting sounds.

"Speak up!" Piotr's voice was heard. Or was it Michael's? Or Hanna's? Its origin escaped them. Music altered its sources. And who was it addressed to? What was the objective? Why was it uttered?

"I'm in pain". And she collapsed.

But the music was relentless.

"For a while now I've been envying the dead, plants, molluscs crawling while being unaware of crawling, a wheel or a foot crushing them whilst they remain unaware still! All that I wished to be". Him.

"I went back for the last time; to ask him once more... hoping! If this had been given to me I would have wanted nothing else; with this expectation, everything else I had hoped for had been extinguished; the greatest victory, the only freedom fit for me, was this slavery. A child! A child of my own! Every dream I had was poured into, overflowing into this obsession! The doctor, polite and cynical as always. "She still hasn't grasped it, poor girl". He had me undergo another general examination, the third in six months. When we finished and he sat behind his desk, he was more polite and diplomatic than ever before, weighing every word, though saying the same things like any other time". Her.

He unlocked his case and randomly pulled out manuscripts, roll films, reels, recorders, flash bulbs, tapes, photometers; he let them fall to the ground right in front of him, a pile of garbage.

"This is what we are!" Him.

With trembling hands he loaded the reel into the device. Then, he lit the motor; it gurgled. The beam hit against furniture and wall, it diffused.

Asian monk. Emptying a can onto his yellow habit; then setting it aflame. The inhuman peace that betrays intolerable pain. The habit is scorched first, then the flesh; for everyone to see, those huddling around with lenses and zooms, with microphones. For his Gods; to have them rescued or to rescue him…

"Instead of a child, I was carrying… The foetus I had hoped for, I had blissfully related to my vomiting and pain… It wasn't a foetus, it wasn't! It was…"

Now every motion slows down, further and further. The music, too. The martyr raises his arms, extends them; they are still, like two burning tapers.

"And it was so beautiful, my life! So very beautiful! Though I never had what I'd been waiting for, I didn't have the child that… It was then, in the absence of motherhood and love I came to realize how full my life was; as long as I was living it, in the way I was living it. Like the splendour of this music within its pause".

Children with dark, distended, hungry eyes, bloated stomachs, swarms of flies hovering above and around them, children surging forward, gesturing, beseeching. Their teeth become exposed. Chattering. There's no sound.

"I hate it; I've always hated malady, always dreamed of something else, the ideal for the overaged and the incurable: euthanasia or instant death during sleep".

"Oh stop it, stop this stupefying music!"

…An entire pack, an ant mound growing bigger and bigger, magnetizing; the stench of burnt flesh; the regurgitation of the flame…

"Since time immemorial!"

"Centuries and centuries ago!"

Now he leans to the side, steaming. And the hungry pack charges forward, hands and voices, mute voices, mania, he wobbles, re-treats, they're hiding him, cover the centre of the square, hide the fire that expands; a wave breaking then bruising. A pyramid . of teeth, eyes, hairless crania.

And the music, merciless, never stops; it gallops; then retreats, falters with them.

An eye within a frozen world; the world within a crushed eye; he paces, what man, what woman, how many? In big empty cities, uninhabited, ancient forests, by land, sea and air, without ever encountering… Nothing but vague and soiled silhouettes of men or animals, of now and then, setting out like meteorites, from afar, satiated, asphyxiated in the line of vision, with their diluted infected figure, only for a moment, a fragment of a moment, before they are swallowed up.

"They begin their life like a promise to live and once they're finished they have left behind them wounds and so much…"

"The iris that whittles".

"Evaporates".

"Enough! This music is murderous!"

"Now I understand Mario Ely. His passion for hashish. A whole suitcase, loaded with it. Customs officers in Malaga grabbed it out of our hands".

No sound, not even a gesture or a single relation. Not even one! None!

"Me! Me! Me!" Her.

She rose and, running, stepped out of the room, fierce, hair di-shevelled; Michael's eye, tireless, followed her, along with his uncontracted music.

...9, 8, 7, 6, 5, 4, 3, 2, 1, 0. An eye opens and shuts. Opens and fades. Opens and drinks.

He raised his glass and drank in one gulp. Bottoms up! Kyros.

And the roving vision, breathless, to touch, to speak, to restore some semblance of contact, a relation, with all the shells hover-ing or so you feel, hovering crowded within the void; now she falters; then again, defeated, she moves slowly, cautiously, pant-ing, charges forward deranged, the tops of tall buildings storm-ing upwards and head on like spearheads, the trees in large rainy forests become detached, uprooted, they swim like green tender fuselages, the waves are reversed, turned upside-down; breath runs out.

"You, if nothing else, have lived your life. You got to meet some-one, Ely, Joseph. You are heading towards nothingness but you set out from something. Whereas I, I..."

...No presence, no presence. None whatsoever...

"I said stop it! I won't have any more of this! I cannot tolerate this music! Stop it or I'll chop off your fingers!"

"Do you know how old I am? At six I was a child, at fourteen a student, a teacher at twenty-five. And aside from my mother's harsh caress, I haven't known... I've lived with the expectation of love..."

"These we offer thee, yours, born of your creations".

"Who will give love?"

"Who has it?"

"And if ever, which I doubt, if ever I'm given love, of grace, though I no longer anticipate it, indeed I'm frightened of it, I won't know how to part with everything I lack".

"My valuable habits!"

"Neither carnal, nor spiritual — no pleasure from anywhere!"

"It's the only thing we've got. The certainty of deprivation for life".

"Avgi, my dearest friend, has showed me the way".

"A comment?"

"Irrationality for the rational ones!"

"For the irrational ones, hope!"

...9, 8, 7, 6, 5, 4, 3, 2, 1, 0...

"The end! The end! Of reek and stench, of virtue and hope".

The next image in slow motion; utter silence; Neil pacing weightless in the crater of Quiet Moon...

"A disgrace!"

Father Stavros jumped up:

"It appears that, in here, the only rational one is me!"

The turn of events spoiled both his appetite and the euphoria he had brought with him. When he saw Maria running outside, eyes red and welled with tears, he didn't try to stop her; patience! He saw Joseph vomiting and he envied him; at least he felt relief! He saw Kyros whimpering and pleading for love; and he was exasperated. All the while, Michael with his guitar and stolidity kept triggering his rage; how he listened and watched, impartial. Just as the other two. The King and Queen of cards!

"That's that..." roared the priest.

But again, no one paid any attention to him.

"Please! Please, may I?" he asked in a stentorian voice.

He took their silence for attention and consent. "Everything we have seen and said, and done– it may well be like that, maybe; I for one, I'm not buying it. But even if it is so, this is just one side of it, the demonical side. Life is so much more than nightmares and evil, pain, death! There's love, love of the child and the woman, of God, there's water, bread, playing, sleep, there are trees, fruit, flowers, mother, father, youth, travels, music — not this music, God forbid! There's the sea and the mountains, the plains and the air, stars and ships, health and wealth, peace, people sacrificing everything for others! There's repentance and serene death in good time! Well? I'm asking you!"

"Yes, there's everything you've said too. All the things that annihilate one another in the grip of all-consuming time!" Akritas replied with the aloofness of an embittered man.

"I'm sorry to say, Joseph, your views have changed tremendously! You used to be undaunted by life! What you just said, and everything before it, is clear denial of God" protested the priest.

"Or acceptance of the only one in existence".

The music stopped. Father Stavros rose to his feet and signalled to his friend; "Time to leave. Enough is enough!" Compliant, Kyros obeyed. No one intervened to try and stop them.

"It's late; tomorrow I will officiate at Matins and mass. For those who do believe".

. . . .

"Yes, time to go", the Dioscurus repeated in his daze. "I'm sorry…"

. . . .

"Goodnight to all".

Only four "goodnights" saw them out.

Maria returned to the room, empty and calm. The Archangielsks got up and, holding her on either side, led her to the high back armchair. They sat opposite her.

Time passed; and no movement or speech was offered to interrupt the progress of anticipation.

Joseph was looking at the dying fire. Embittered.

The Archangielsks were looking at Michael with respect and parental love.

Michael, hermetic, in the world whence he had drawn his music.

Outside, the pendulum clock set out on a new melodious count; the youth stood up and gently placed the guitar next to Joseph's folded legs; then, he walked slowly, passing by the Archangielsks, and stood over Maria. He looked into her eyes persistently. The last beat of the clock resounded from the hall. Midnight. The count began anew. Maria lifted her head and looked straight into his eyes, her gaze a blend of decisiveness and challenge.

"You can!" he told her. "If you have love!"

She said "I can" and propped herself up; her eyes inviting him.

Joseph had wanted to crawl between them, cut them off; but the two steps that separated him from them seemed like a long way, strenuous and pointless. He stood still, hovering, until the Archangielsks, holding him up just as they had done with Maria a while ago, led him out into the moonlit snowed yard, both of them silent and respectful.

From inside the living room, as the two became one, he heard their asthmatic, redeeming voices:

"When?"

"Always now".

ON SUNDAY SHE WOKE TO A BRIGHT, WHITE WORLD.

And the sun that came out just for a bit, as the bells tolled for Doxology, was splintered into innumerable crystals.

After the *apolysis* of the divine liturgy and the commemoration of the dead, the snowfall resumed and carried on all day and until noon of the next.

The last bus arrived at Spilia on Monday afternoon, its only passengers being Miss Ioulia Michaelidou, Avgi's replacement, three students attending the Solea High School and two workers of the Forestry Department.

One hour later, a second bus and Lefteris' taxi, Lefteris being Father Stavros' son-in-law, had had to drive back to Kakopetria when just a hundred meters beyond the curve to Spilia and Kourdali, they discovered that the rural gravel road had caved in, causing a serious risk of landslide.

Notified by the two fretted drivers, the police sergeant alerted Nicosia so that the relevant announcement be made on the radio. He also tried to contact the leaders of the adjacent villages, but the only available telephones, at the community offices and the forestry department, were dead.

He quickly loaded a few warning signs onto the jeep, and aided by his assistant, fitted the non-skid chains onto the car tires and drove on slowly, carefully checking the main road to Karvounas and Troodos, down to the curve to Spilia.

The road sign was totally covered in snow; they cleared it away and placed two additional signs – "X-Landslide" and "X-Risk of Subsidence" – where they could be easily seen, and a third warning sign fifty meters ahead, on the gravel road.

Within the fifteen minutes it took them to place the signs, three cars heading to Spilia had had to turn back; the first, a small two-door car driven by an intern lawyer at Serghides and Fardis Legal Office who, by his own word, was delivering an urgent message for "someone" in the village. The second, a red Lotus convertible. Its owner, a tanned young man, fittingly bundled up in his sports jacket and fur Kazakh cap, protested over the condition of the streets and, in response to the sergeant's eager offer to help him, spat out a "thank you", said he had a personal affair to tend to, and returned back to the main road to Nicosia, fountains of snow spurting out from behind and in front of his car tyres.

"Do you know who that was?" the lawyer smiled, not without envy. "His name is Marios Orphanos, the son of the well-known business magnate; a playboy".

The third driver arrived just as the police jeep was setting out to return to the station. He was a bearded man in his seventies, driving a pre-war Ford, well-preserved on the outside, though its engine panted as if suffering from incurable asthma. A doctor from Nicosia, he had been summoned to Evrychou Hospital for an emergency and thought it a fine opportunity to visit a couple, friends of his, in Spilia.

"I'm afraid, as you may well see for yourself…" the sergeant explained. "Even with snow chains, I would advise against it".

"When do you think the road will open?" the doctor asked, ominously scratching his beard.

"Who knows? It depends on the weather. We'll make the announcement as soon as it's been repaired".

For five days, until Friday, the snow kept piling up, with breaks of an hour or two over every 24 hour period. And the cold, during those breaks, was polar. Reparations on the street began as late as the middle of the second week.

In the meantime, no one had been able to leave the twin villages, nor had any of the Spilia residents managed to return to the village on foot, lodging instead in larger villages nearby.

The only exception was reported by three Telecommunications workers who'd been struggling for days to locate the damage to the phone line. From a distance, they saw an unknown man, wearing a fleece hood and a leather jacket, walking along the edge of the cliff. They called out to him, asked him where he was heading and if he needed any help; he waved something, probably uttered a greeting, but they heard nothing.

No, he was quite far from them, at the bottom of the valley, and they were working high up the hill, they couldn't make out who he was.

"Was he going to the village?"

"No, he was coming down from there. Probably coming down".

"Dear members of the Committee! First of all I would like to thank you for responding to my invitation so eagerly. The reason I have convened this extraordinary meeting is that, as you very well know, God willing and weather permitting, our School is hopefully scheduled to open after the conclusion of this act of God, and a decision must be made on the matter set forth by Mr Demetriades during our previous meeting last Thursday. So, to cut a long story short, I will now read the minutes prepared by dear Kyros".

Father Stavros put on his glasses.

"It has been suggested by the Chairman, the reverend Father Stavros Alexandrinos, that the Prayer of the Cyclamens be henceforth dedicated to the salvation of Mr and Ms Akritas. During the discussion that followed the suggestion, the following views were set forth: First, the Chairman underlined that, seeing as the principle of joint prayer has been successfully applied for years now, it must also be similarly applied to the case of the Akritases who, as the Chairman has personally observed, are in need of enlightenment and aid from above. 'The daily prayer of the seven children squads will enfold them in a shield of faith and heal them of physical and mental pain'. The second view put forward by the Secretary, Mr Demetriades, was that if the aforementioned principle was to be applied to this particular case, then both the Committee and the institution would instigate the likely wrath of the couple in question, causing damage instead of producing a benefit, whilst exacerbating what they intended to heal".*

Father Stavros then addressed the other three members:

"So, madam and gentlemen, your views please".

The Community President, the Church Board Officer and the recently appointed member, Avgi's replacement, opted not to speak. They had already expressed their opinions during the first and second meetings convened to this end. The views of both the Chairman and the Secretary were equally strong and it was difficult to decide which one to adopt.

"Whatever you decide, reverend, we will sign", the Community President replied to the Chairman's second, more intense appeal, expressing the opinion of the other two members as well.

"If this is how you put it, then the case is closed", Father Stavros said. "The President has the winning vote".

"The majority of one", Demetriades smiled, defeated, and added: "Allow me, in any case, to remind you of what I exhaustively set forth during our previous meeting, the profound discontent expressed the other day by Ms Akritas over the prayer of the cyclamens".

"Excuse me, dear man", Father Stavros interrupted him, "this is irrelevant and insubstantial. The reaction of our dear Maria, or of anyone else for that matter, should be of no concern to us. This is a matter of principle; it either applies to all or none. Of course, if you wish to request that the Committee Charter be changed, please feel free; provided that you submit your request in writing and well in advance".

Kyros Demetriades did not answer. In the end, he had to confess to himself that the priest was right; it was and remained a matter of principle. And he was certainly ill prepared to raise such a question. Even if he did take the risk, the decision would only be made in a minimum of two or three weeks.

He bowed his head over his notes, sensing the priest's pretentious hawk-like gaze piercing him, in anticipation of a typical confirmation of his victory. It was precisely then that he heard his new colleague's fine, somewhat tawny voice. He fixed his eyes upon her, avoiding looking towards the Chairman.

"As I am the most recent member of the Committee, the articles of the Charter are still fresh in my memory. Therefore, I do believe that Article No 23 will indeed help us to tackle this issue in the most anodyne manner. Allow me to read from the Charter:"During the aforementioned 'prayers of the cyclamens', supplications will be made in favour of members of the community that are suffering, ill and in distress"etc. To the best of my knowledge, Mr and Ms Akritas are not members of the community. They are not even permanent residents of Spilia".

"After all", Miss Michaelides resumed after a brief pause, "there's no reason why we shouldn't advise the members of the Cyclamens to pray and commemorate the Akritases in silence, both during the joint morning prayer and privately, at home".

And she sat down.

Kyros Demetriades looked at her with gratitude; in spite of her broad nose, straight hair and old-fashioned eye glasses, Miss Michaelides suddenly appeared to him very agreeable, indeed more than agreeable; if she improved her appearance a bit, changed eyeglasses and hairstyle, she could definitely be attractive. After all, in spite of initial indications, she proved to be smart and methodical!

He grinned at her. She responded with an awkward smile and leant over her notes.

The other members were now staring at the Chairman, who had opened the Charter, and was browsing over it.

Once Father Stavros had finished reviewing the articles, he removed his glasses and spoke again:

"Miss Michaelides has resolved the dilemma for us", he confessed with concealed relief. "And, in fact, without any violation of our principles. Indeed! According to the Charter, we are not obliged to commemorate the Akritases, nor Miss Avgi, who is also a non-native resident of Spilia-Kourdali. The word 'native' bothers me, Kyros. We should change it".

"With pleasure, Mr Chairman".

"I also agree with the view that there's no reason not to commemorate them in silence, without setting off these extremely thin-skinned individuals, if I may say so! Or, even better, we could leave the door open and review our decision, if they too should agree to the prayer. I will take it upon myself to see where they stand. Again, kudos to you, Miss Michaelides!"

Once the meeting was adjourned and the others set out for a

glass of *zivania* at the "Lovely Spilia", Kyros Demetriades gave credit to Ioulia.

"Bravo! Congratulations", he told her. "Thank you very much. We've just defied my dearest Father Stavros".

They switched off the lights, put on their rubber boots, locked the doors and stepped out onto the snowy street.

"Is their condition as serious as people say?" Miss Michaelides asked.

"I don't know! I suppose... Perhaps".

"What about Miss Avgi? What was she like?" the young teacher asked again.

"A misfit".

"A misfit?" she repeated. He had misinterpreted her question. "I meant that..."

"Yes!" Kyros interrupted her line of thought. "She didn't fit into this setting... Just as the Archangielsks and the Akritases and all of you who..."

"Just like you too!" she stated with a confidence which flattered him.

"Me? My dear, I fit like a glove. I am Spilia!"

The sun had begun to set and the snow on the top of Hionistra was breathing in purple hues.

She felt no remorse over what had happened; nor did she feel ashamed in hindsight for the manner in which it had occurred. Ordinarily, looking at him so corroded, she should have felt guilty and needed to clear things up– plainly and sincerely tell him that what had taken place was what she had wanted to take place, that it had all started purely and nicely, and had ended unforgettably. And also, that she was sorry on his behalf, for not having tried enough to give her – and take for himself – so much happiness from a single act, an act that for years now they had been performing as an arduous quest of pleasure, though never admitting to it, and never as an initiation into the only completeness there is.

Finally, she would tell him that, if he still so wished, she would not object to a divorce; if, however, for the few months she had left to live, he preferred that they continued living together, she had no objection to that either– as long as she'd be free to see Michael, to receive or visit the Archangielsks. Still, she never told him, and she knew deep down that she never would, unless obliged. She could feel it, she was no longer willing to do what she'd normally do in the past. The night of the Archangielsks pushed her out of orbit, an orbit that wasn't normal, how could it be – and into a new one that had at its core the erotic explosion that had transpired within her and was still causing ripples from cell to cell and origin to origin, from day to day, like a wonderful rumination.

He wasn't wrathful and humiliated over what had happened; or the manner in which it had occurred. Ordinarily, he should have felt furious at allowing himself to be swayed into an untimely and clumsy reaction that had exposed his soul's most unspoken depths; and at the tolerance he showed in dealing with that unforgivable insult that had been carried out against him, in his own house! And everything that followed it; the pleading and the sighing and the squeaking, her panting, and that long, so piercing ultimate cry of relief, self-sufficiency and redemption that rose from within her body and reverberated inside the entire house. Normally, he should have kicked her out or left her that very same night; or, if he was magnanimous and civilized, do so after demanding an explanation from her. Regardless of the errors and omissions he might have made, she had no right to disgrace him like that. But had she? Had what happened really debased him? These were the only feelings he didn't seem to have; in fact, for everything he said and everything that followed his ridiculous explosions, hers and the others', he felt relieved, not humiliated or wrathful. The most vivid sentiment that overwhelmed him was surprise at himself and the boundaries of his tolerance, his indifference. If he kept quiet, it was because he was waiting for her to make the decision as to whether to leave or stay. He had already talked to her long before the night of the Archangielsks. Now all he wanted was more time to ponder over his ideas, formulated into prickly shapes by his mature wrath, and rearrange the feelings that had made them rise to the surface. To make sure of the extent of his alienation and unhappiness in order to put an end to this cumbersome experience. Once and for all!

And so she watched him stir the ashes and keep quiet; the "Labyrinth" he never once reopened. For several days now he hadn't driven back to Nicosia in search of Avgi; nor had he gone to the post office in quest of a letter or any other document that could help him trace her. He hadn't even gone to the Police to push, accuse and make threats. She observed him stealthily and started to believe that all his spiritual and biological functions were either inert or lethargic, that he had grown old from one night to the next; and every attempt on her part to help him or to provoke him, violently even, to find, to regain himself, his true and frightful and fierce self that, on the night of the Archangielsks, was promptly revealed prowling in the depths of the swamp – or at least his old egocentric self, though not what she was now looking for; what she found out in the course of that unprecedented erotic fulfilment – the self as an agleam voracious being equipped with indefinite reserves of joy and elation, even in the grip of lethal danger, she couldn't achieve it. He was a tame, irresponsive vegetable that had irrevocably condemned itself!

And so he watched her sitting on the ground, feet crossed on the fleece carpet, absent-mindedly stroking the chords of the guitar that had been left there, forgotten since that night, and he felt no urge to rise from his own dilemma, his Symplegades, in order to release her from hers, or to help her finally reach a decision, any decision!

As for her, she knew (he must have felt it too) that time, passing at her expense, galloping – time belonged to her; it was her responsibility and she would finally need to decide to either use or be divested of it – only her! Then again, why? To what avail? A couple of days more or less, either won or lost, do not really matter amidst the helplessness of a predesignated shipwreck.

But no; lo and behold! She made a decision... some kind of a decision. Her face became alive with the purpose that so unexpectedly filled her. She would always put herself first!

She got up, went to the portmanteau, threw a coat over her shoulders, donned a knit cap and put on her gloves.

"I'm going", she told him.

She grabbed hold of the guitar.

"Are you coming back?"

"It's not up to me".

Hanna Archangielsk opened the door for her. Piotr was working in the back room they had turned into an office; every day at this hour he recorded his notes for the day's work, along with general observations that could prove useful at some point.

"He's almost done", Hanna told her. "Have a seat", she added and pointed to the only proper chair in the room, a high-backed chair, identical to the one Maria was sitting on when Michael got up and stood in front of her. The colour was their only difference. Hers was painted black, dressed in gilded tapestry. This one here was bright white. Bare. Of wood and colour.

Hanna took a seat on a stool, next to her, identical to hers, only white.

She glanced across the room; books and magazines all around, and the harpsichord. It was a long sunlit room, furnished with books, just as described to her. But this picture, though graphically conveying the first and foremost impression, was incomplete; apart from the books, the harpsichord, the fireplace, what struck her the most was the ambience in the room. Something of the chapel's proud barrenness had been transferred here; something of the austerity, asceticism and economy of the wall-paintings had perched upon the space and its residents. Oh, the humbleness and frugality of spiritual people, the youthfulness hidden in their white hair! Like those figures half-buried in plaster. "A sunroom furnished with..." She couldn't find the end of the sentence. Or perhaps she could but dared not add it.

Instead, she turned her attention to a pile of books close to her: "Das Kapital", "Les fleurs du mal", "History of two critical Byzantine centuries", "The Archangels of Fire", "Architecture", "The art of dance as a means of awakening focal energy", "Avatar", "Cypriot Erotica", "Bhagavad Gita".

"You read a lot!" she said, to initiate conversation.

"Much less than I would like", Hanna smiled.

"And each book in a different language! I imagine you have no trouble reading them, speaking so many languages as you do!"

"We have a friend who's a fluent speaker of more languages! Still, he says there are many great works he hasn't been able to read yet".

"Aren't they available in translation? I mean the books you're interested in?"

"None of the unique works have been translated; they are thankfully untranslatable!"

She was silent for a while and then:

"I soon intend to start learning Turkish. We're going to Cappadocia and Pontus next".

"Then it's a fine opportunity. And, I guess, an antidote to boredom".

Hanna offered her a glass of wine.

"We usually don't have time to be bored; the truth is we like it here in Spilia; we like nature, our work and the people".

Maria saw that her conventional questions were essentialized by Hanna's answers, opening pathways to issues she cared not discuss at the moment, so she decided to go on and bluntly state what it was that had led her to their upper floor, the *anoi,* indifferent to the consequences this act of hers would have on her ground floor, the *katoi:* to ask after Michael. They hadn't seen each other since Saturday night and she yearned to meet him again, listen to his music, his voice. In fact, knowing Hanna and Piotr as she did, she was certain she could, perhaps should, speak openly about her thoughts and feelings for their hermetic guest.

She brought the glass of wine to her lips; the bright burgundy liquid spilled inside her like living matter, vibrating, making her feel her tongue, palate and chest clear and translucent.

She placed the guitar upon the "Two Byzantine centuries".

"He forgot it", she said. "I came here to bring it back. Can you please call him?"

"Michael's gone".

"When...?"

"On Saturday night".

"For how..."

"I don't know! Nobody does".

"Didn't he leave a...?"

"They never do".

. . . .

"Won't he...?"

. . . .

Perhaps, she replied; perhaps, she explained; perhaps. Maria heard nothing. All the happiness, the euphoria she had been feeling for days now, the warmth, the unexpected —was now annihilated. It wasn't just her soul that was paralyzed but her entire muscular system. She tried to get up, but she couldn't move.

"Maria".

She felt Hanna leaning over her, her proximity too warm to tolerate, talking to her, asking her. Then, Piotr, too cold to tolerate next to Hanna. She tried to understand what was happening to her; it was no use. Their speech was soundless, signless, it was a hollow blinking of the eyes, grimaces, their gestures pointless movements in the light, the orbits of two dark, extinguished forms...

She tried to react, to become revived by crying or yelling; all she did was make sure she herself was no longer in position to communicate — neither inwardly nor outwardly; to think or feel hurt; not even that. Within an infinitesimal moment, her metamorphosis had begun — perhaps had even been completed, she didn't know yet; she acquired the properties of an inanimate. See this sharp paper cutter here? If she was to plunge it into her flesh, she had no doubt that chlorophyll and a milky resined liquid would pour out. Still, what was happening to her could be the conclusion of a process which...

Before she reached the heart of zero, before losing all remnants of her human nature, she felt a bulge at the lower part of her torso, just above the pool of blood, not hers, the blood she had sipped a moment ago, just above the area from whence sprouted her two long, motionless roots.

The voices she heard in the fog; doused her like something akin to cold water. She was in pain, her stomach seemingly fixed to her chest.

"Sir?"

"I'm her husband, Joseph Akritas".

"I'm Dr Herodotou, how do you do? What did you ask just now?"

"Why won't she come round?"

"Don't worry, she will, soon I hope. Both Ms Akritas and the foetus are just fine; I see no reason for concern".

"I'm asking because she has... I only recently found out myself".

"Yes, she did confide it to me. She felt awkward, guilty. She hid it from you whilst you were abroad. I suppose your in-laws told you. No? Anyway, they brought her here. Yes, I did contact your family physician. He has called on her; he too believes everything will go smoothly. Thankfully she hasn't reached the final stage of the disease. This is indeed consoling! With alternative therapy and the rest I do hope we'll suspend deterioration so that she'll have a normal pregnancy".

"What you just said, is it an expectation or a prediction?"

"It's an expectation. I can't make safe predictions regarding the development of her health, or her pregnancy. We have a difficult case on our hands".

"May I sit down?"

"By all means!"

. . . .

The pause that followed the stichomythia in her room at the "Hygeia" Polyclinic went on for a while; for hours, perhaps days. With a sense of bliss she could feel the warmth of the smooth sheet over her body, of silence upon her spirit. The vast dark-ness, yes!, if she could see it in colour, the sheet upon her would be sleek and opaque. And the words that dotted it, small tinted stains flickering across it all the time, reflections of an unknown world, ultrasensitive folds, depending on the whims and deflec-tions of light.

Until the moment...

She half-opened her eyes, just enough to hide that she was look-ing at him. He sat opposite her, hands on his knees, looking at the city through the open window, with the same stereotypical, icy expression he bore while staring at the fireplace the other day. If she could hate, she would... If she could slap, she would... If she could erase him from her body and her memory, she...

What she could still do was speak. Yes, this she felt she could do! She had one more weapon. She still felt strong. And malicious!

She opened her eyes and stirred to catch his eye; then, she spoke:

"It's theirs and I'm having it".

. . . .

"There's no way I'll allow any of you to stand in its way".

. . . .

"I thought he'd abandoned me, without so much as leaving a note, not even a typical..."

. . . .

"But no... For as long as I'm alive he'll be here... here, inside me. Not just near me or around me, dispersed, not just on my epidermis or my offshoots. At the core!"

. . . .

"I loved him, gave myself to him. He infiltrated me from the first moment he touched the chords. The sounds had sunk into my chest, like a web, overwhelming me. He is and I am..."

....

"I'm no longer envious of any woman or man. I've stopped crying over... over my youth, my talent, the nights I was buried loveless in your bed".

....

"I'm no longer afraid. I was afraid before, before collecting what I have collected, what all of you will never collect in a lifetime!"

....

"In a single cry!"

"Please, Mr Akritas, you must step outside", another female voice was heard, or was it a male voice? – from the other side of the white chamber, behind the screen. "The patient must rest now. Dr Herodotou will tell you everything you want to know, perhaps later today. Right now he's presiding at the medical council convened extraordinarily for Ms Akritas".

"Has she fallen back into a coma?"

"No, I gave her sedatives. I didn't want her to hear the views of the medical council. She'll come to within twenty minutes".

"Good!"

"Her pulse?"

"Normal".

"Pressure?"

"Likewise".

"When she was brought here by the two strangers, she had hypotension".

"Can I please see her blood test? And the charts? Hmm! X-rays?"

"Nurse, can you please bring the X-rays?"

"I suggest we give her multivitamins".

"I'm not so sure. Of course, they can't do any harm either".

"The idea of curettage has been definitively rejected?"

"Rejected by her; and categorically so, even though I explained in great length…"

"Then?"

"I fear the same. Let's be hopeful…"

"Do you think she'll make it to labour?"

"I'm not a pessimist. In fact, if in this case I had been as optimistic as I usually am, I would have said there are some faint hopes. So far there's no indication of a relapse".

"Nevertheless, there is no guarantee, especially given the additional physical encumbrance".

"This is my own concern too, gentlemen. I'm afraid the only thing left for us to do is keep our fingers crossed!"

"There's something else I've been wanting to ask. What's her mental state?"

"I can't really tell. For quite a long time now she's been in a comatose state, an unusual type of coma. I would term it as an eclipse of the senses. It's the first time I've come across it, a kind of conscious sleep! Here are the X-rays".

"Hmm... yes..."

"Just as I assumed. Fine, this is a good thing! Though no one can really give assurances as to the extent of..."

"Can I have another look please?"

"Do you observe?"

"Certainly! Amazing!"

"Are you referring to the bright meniscus? Around the damaged cells?"

"These types of cells..."

"Precisely! They give the impression of radioactive..."

"I wouldn't say radioactive! Rather... no, this is not the right word. However..."

"What are you inferring?"

"It's still too soon. This... meniscus here is befuddling. It reverses all given facts — or at least, alters them. It could just be a side effect. Either that or we're dealing with something new, either salvaging or mortal".

"The unknown siding with the malignant".

"What I'm about to say may be criticized as a non-scientific hypothesis, but I'll risk it; this radiation or whatever anyone wishes to term it, may come from a possible peak of the body's defensive activity. It could be a form of reaction, a kind of armature!"

"Maybe so; in fact, may it be so! For the time being, the only certain thing is that we're faced with a new situation, an influx of unknown facts for which only assumptions may be formulated".

"If Dr Herodotou's hypothesis is correct…"

"We'll know in a few weeks. Perhaps the new blood test will enlighten us…"

"…"

"In any case, it's quite comical! We're incapable of reacting! Ignorant! It's one of those cases where I realize the vanity of our every effort. We're only curing what may be self-cured if we draw back and leave it to nature to deal with it. More or less!"

"Truly, a unique case! One in a million, or even rarer! A few weeks ago I gave her a life expectancy of about nine months. Whereas today, in nine months from now, she'll be giving birth! And also… this!"

"Life in the tomb… And post-mortem pathologists become obstetricians!"

"It's a good thing the patient cannot hear us".

"Are you sure she can't?"

"Don't worry. As I said, she'll wake up in twenty minutes from now. At exactly 11.15".

"I believe we can call it a day now, gentlemen".

"Of course. Don't forget – drinks at Hippocrates tonight".

She didn't wake up at 11.15. She was fully alert from the beginning to the end of the meeting, in a state of "anodyne and conscious coma" as aptly put by one of them, Dr Herodotou perhaps, she wasn't sure. The pills that were intended to put her to sleep she hid in her dressing gown when the nurse was going over the charts. She kept them for an emergency! She had collected five by now. With eight or ten...

"I came to take you home", he told her and reached out his hand to help her get out of bed.

"I can get up on my own".

She stood up, leant against the bed's metallic frame.

He helped her put on her coat, brought her cap and gloves, assisted her with her rubber boots. She accepted his care with apathy that gave him the illusion he was still useful to her.

"I'm going back to Spilia", she told him.

"So am I".

As they were coming down the stairs from the mezzanine floor, he offered her his free hand. She took it. They walked to the taxi that was parked at the entrance to the Polyclinic. The taxi driver took the small suitcase from Akritas and placed it in the boot.

"I didn't come with the Deux Chevaux. I'm having trouble concentrating these days", he said. "I thought it'd be better for us to take a taxi".

They sat down and the driver started the engine.

"Does the gentleman know?" she asked.

Akritas nodded yes.

"To Spilia, aka the Cave, madam!" the driver said upon hearing her question and, taking a slow turn, left the busy road in front of the Clinic to enter the main road to the airport.

"It's a Cave, really", she whispered to herself. Then, aloud, she told Akritas: "So you knew…"

"I assumed as much".

She looked straight into his eyes for the first time after that night. Inquisitively.

"So…"

"Yes! Always".

They kept quiet for a while. Then he spoke:

"If I could, I would love it".

"You're not obliged to".

"I know; but I would have wanted it. I'm afraid I understand and accept much more than I can. Perhaps this is the beginning. But it's not entirely impossible that it is also the end".

There was silence, again. Once out of the city and on the highway, the driver accelerated and put a cassette into the car radio.

"Bambakaris!" he exclaimed.

Akritas kindly asked him to lower the volume.

"I can switch it off if it bothers you", the man eagerly replied.

"No, just keep the volume down".

"D' you fancy music?" the driver insisted. "It's my greatest joy really! Football and Greek popular music, *rebetika* as well. I have some foreign tunes too, if that's your thing".

"No", Akritas answered.

"We like music. Especially Greek music", Maria said in a soft voice. "In fact, there was a time when…"

Bambakaris was succeeded by Tsitsanis, then Papaioannou and Zambettas. Then her voice, in a crescendo over the *bouzouki:*

"Has there been a return?"

He didn't reply immediately.

"Not yet", he said after a while, interpreting her question at will. "The police fears she's been kidnapped by a professional; or that she has run away. Unless she left the country with a fake passport, which I find highly unlikely".

"Any letter or message?"

"Nothing but her pay check and a few circulars. I understand they've appointed a replacement. I only found out yesterday".

"I wasn't asking about her..." she told him.

He turned and looked into her eyes.

"Yes, I know".

The dog welcomed her with a merry grunt; it bent its legs, crawled on its belly and rubbed his nose over her knees and hands.

"The most sincere welcome..." she whispered.

The rack was loaded with beech wood; white roses in the vase.

"Who lit the fire?" she asked, her palms spread over the fireplace.

"Nicodemus' daughter will be coming here to help you. She's good at housekeeping and cooking. The soup must be ready".

He went to the kitchen, to check.

Maria sat down and pulled the flowers close to her. She brought them near her face and, without taking a breath, let their fine aroma permeate her. A sense of purity spread inside her.

"Egg lemon soup!" Akritas exclaimed, returning to the living room, in a brave effort to be courteous and natural. "It's first class! She's a gem, that girl. Rodi! Little Rodi. You'll like her".

She didn't reply, for fear of dispersing the transparent languor set within her by the aroma.

"Are you tired? Would you rather lie down?" he asked.

"No, I'm fine", she had to answer. "Thank you! For the roses".

"It wasn't me". And he went on, without showing he was bothered by her preference for anything that was not done or tended by him. "I'm puzzled actually, it's not their season. We're still three months ahead of spring".

"It must be…"

"I guess… This variety doesn't grow here. They must have made a special order in Nicosia".

She offered no comment. She turned to the dog that had crawled to her feet, wagging its snowy tail with sheer joy. She whispered softly, just enough so she could be heard:

"And this, an even more sincere welcome!"

Rodi, shy, walked into the room to say hello and inform them that the table had been set. She was sixteen, with rosy cheeks, braids, rough fingers and eyes the colour of chocolate, perpetually lowered.

"Thank you, Rodi".

Late in the afternoon, in spite of Joseph's reasonable objections, she insisted on testing her strength with a short walk. She took the quiet alley that led to the church of Panaghia of Arakas. The sun dispersed into rosy hues, painting the fluffs of clouds over the white curvatures of Madari and Chionistra.

The apple and peach trees were covered in a downing of crystalized leafage; with the evening light cast upon them, the leaves gleamed and trembled, emitting a soft rustling all around.

The river, flowing among poplars and rocks, sent shivers across the valley.

Her boots were sunk into the snow to a depth of about the width of a hand, following the fresh footraces of a hare that had treaded the same path in search of grass or shelter.

She moved slowly, trying to put her thoughts into some kind of order, to find a way to reconcile the irreconcilable that alternated light with darkness within her: the bliss for the new life she could feel growing roots inside her, and her disgraceful panic against the surrounding threats: How aptly the doctor had summarized what was happening to her: "life in the tomb!"... The utter contradiction! The post-mortem pathologist was at the same time an obstetrician! And amidst millions of women, she was the receptacle of the unexplainable that perplexed those great men of science. She was indeed a special case!

She heard a rustle; something akin to crawling. She paused. From the snow-covered bushes along the edges of the path, the hare emerged. No, it was a rabbit; a stark black rabbit with a white spot on its forehead, sprinkled with snow water. Without cowardice, despite its nature, the animal approached her. It bent its legs, crawled on its belly and tucked its snout between her boots.

She bowed to caress it. The animal shuddered with cold and expectation. Or...

"What do you want?" she asked as she lifted it close to her chest. "Are you hungry?"

The motion of bowing confirmed her frailty. A sensation of vertigo, loss of balance, came upon her and she let her whole weight lean against the bark of a nut tree. The return home would be cumbersome, it would verify his objections. It was then she heard the roaring. From the depths of the gorge, along with swarms of wild pigeons scattering, there arose the thundering of an engine, spreading out. The rabbit took a fright. She held it tight, calmed it.

It was the Lotus, fitted with non-skid chains, its strong headlights on, even though the sun was yet to set.

Happy to see him, she waved warmly.

"Hi there!"

"Hello!"

He jumped out of the car and walked to her.

"Are you out for a hunt?"

"Are you?"

His laughter was ennobled by vague melancholy.

"How did you discover me?"

"I passed by the house you live in, your friend the teacher's house. I asked a kid and he told me. Will you keep walking or can I give you a ride?" And he laughed at recalling their first dialogue at the pastry shop.

"Like back then?" she returned his smile. "It's late. I should get back".

"Very well! Can I accompany you, either on foot or by car?"

"I'm tired. I'd rather you drove".

"Great! Though I would like to have a chat with you".

"We can chat at home".

"It's crowded. You have guests".

"There must be one empty room".

"What about Mr Akritas?"

"It's of no concern to him".

"I'm sorry to insist, but I would prefer it if we went somewhere else. If it doesn't bother you..."

"Alright! We can sit in the car".

The interior of the Lotus was pleasantly warm, the seats wide and comfortable.

"So?" she encouraged him to speak.

He hesitated for a minute; lit a cigarette. What he was keeping for the end of their conversation was now becoming the prelude...

"I wanted to apologize", he said.

"You, apologize?"

"For what I said and contemplated. Back then". He waited for her to interrupt him, ask something to make it easier on him; she didn't. "I was convinced you were responsible for that stupid incident. You're going to laugh, but I assumed you were frigid or..."

"Or?"

"Nothing; nonsense. The important thing is what I know now".

"And what do you know?"

"If anyone is frigid, it's me. Even in the past, with girls I mean, when I did better… That incident between the two of us was the measure of the failure of every earlier success".

"So I was the reason you were shorn of a beautiful illusion!"

"And I'm grateful for that. Of course, it wasn't easy, having to admit a few things to myself. I was tortured by the dilemma of whether to see you again or not. As you can see, I found it impossible to resist. On my first attempt, the road was closed. The second time, the day before yesterday, you were rushed to the clinic. I almost killed myself, driving from Spilia back to Nicosia. A doctor said you were fine, soon to be released. I went to the Club and bought everyone drinks!"

"They lied to you. I'm never going to be alright. As for your remorse and your other conclusions, they're groundless. If there was anyone taking advantage, it wasn't you. I had used you as an antidote, something to hold on to".

"What you're saying…" he resumed, but she cut in.

"In other words, it was I who was remorseful and repentant. You were the victim. And if you wanted to see me again so that we could talk, I wanted the same twice as much; to apologize".

"But I'm not here just to talk to you, Maria, just to apologize", he exclaimed, following the tone of familiarity she had set from the start of their conversation. "Above everything else, I wanted to tell you how I feel about you; kindly ask you to promise, if you ever feel you want something from someone, from the most superficial thing to… to love, you should know that I… Can you see how changed I am? Those who know me think I've fallen ill or something".

"I've changed too since the last time we met. The 'frigid' one has known love. It's Michael, the young man you saw with the two foreigners. I'm expecting his child!"

He smoked his cigarette to the last puff and threw it out onto the snow. It was a while before they spoke again. What had been said was still pulsating within the closed car.

"What about your illness?" he managed to utter first. "I know about it, Maria... Is there anything that can be done?"

"What could be done has already been done!"

"Are you sure? Perhaps I could help? Anything. I mean, if nothing else... No, I don't mean that, not like that".

"I'm afraid not".

"What about me, Maria? What will become of me?"

"Keep on loving!"

"Loving who? Who is worth it?"

"All the incurable ones. If you look closely, you'll know".

"Can I at least hope?"

"That I'll love you? But I do love you. You are dear to me, I confide in you and I do want to see you. But that's all I can give you. Nothing else!"

He started the engine. Before the car became unstuck from the snow, she drew him close to her and kissed his lips. He made a desperate move, to wrap her in his arms, but held back at the last minute.

"I'm already taken!" she said.

The house was full of people. Father Stavros, the presbytera and

their youngest daughter Leoni, wife to Lefteris, the village's bus
and taxi driver, who brought along her baby in a stroller; Kyros
Demetriades, Ioulia Michaelidou, the Community President, the
police sergeant, Nicodemus.

They welcomed her in choral exclamation, like an ancient chorus.
"It's neither a tragedy, nor a comedy", Maria thought, defeated
and unready to deal with the attack, "It's actually both in my case;
it's a tragicomedy". Along with their wishes for "a healthy pregnancy" and "easy delivery", they also offered her their gifts: the
priest and his wife gave her smoked ham and a jar of traditional
almond dessert. Leoni gave her a set of pink baby clothes because,
she said, she had dreamt that the Akritas' would have a girl. Kyros Demetriades brought the book of a well-known gynaecolo-
gist on pregnant women, containing questions about pregnancy
and the hygiene of the foetus. Miss Michaelidou brought a blue
hand-knitted baby shawl with matching mittens. Nicodemus offered a mat of red fleece. The Community President brought a
splinter from the Holy Cross – "He says he brought it from the
Holy Sepulchre thirty years ago, forever solving the trouble of
buying gifts for weddings and christenings", according to the evil
tongues. The sergeant offered a crude Christ head, carved into
cork, recovered from the swag of a thief defeated by his grand-
father, the most famous "mulazim" in the region. Rodi brought
her eagerness to tend to the unexpected guests, which proved
inadequate against so many friendly voices given to a barrage
of ordering: sweets and lemonades, whisky and wine. "It's one
thing to be eager and another to be trained", the sergeant whispered to Demetriades, when he saw the whisky he had ordered
being served to the priest.

Cornered in his own house, Joseph Akritas was struggling to conceal his discontent over this disorderly invasion. In the end, unable to tolerate the pandemonium caused by the toasting and the
laughing and the well-wishing, he escaped from the living room,

claiming he wanted to prepare something impromptu for the *oinopotes*, the "wine drinkers", as he told the scholarly Demetriades.

"That's a good man!" the priest applauded him. "Did you think you'd get away with a few drinks?"

"Indeed, the occasion calls for clinking glasses", Nicodemus concurred.

"I can help, I'm good at this sort of thing", the priest offered and followed Joseph to the kitchen. Rodi was trying to prepare a new round of drinks.

"Something light", Father Stavros said. "No need to overdo it!"

"Chicken? And some canned food?" asked the deeply trapped host. And he instructed Rodi to kill a hen and steam it.

"Can you do that?" he asked her.

Rodi waved "child's play" and ran outside.

"The girl can slay and scrap a sow in no time, she won't falter before some fowl!" the priest commented.

Joseph Akritas opened two cans, a can of beef and a can of cocktail sausages. He emptied them onto a platter; on a smaller plate he placed a medley of dried nuts: figs, peanuts, roasted chickpeas. While doing that, he emptied half a dozen eggs into a frying pan. Then, he cut the smoked ham into thin slices and served them on celery leaves.

"You're quite good at it, I'll give you that", Father Stavros praised him.

"This will do for now", Akritas said, "until the chicken's ready".

Rodi stepped into the room. Instead of a hen, she proudly clutched a black rabbit from the ears. The poor thing was kicking madly, stretching and shrinking, in a vain effort to break free.

"Where did you find that?" Akritas asked her.

"In the chicken shed".

"It's not ours", he lashed out at her. "Take it back. And do only as I tell you!"

"But it's a wild rabbit, sir", Rodi whimpered.

"The girl is right", Father Stavros certified. "No one in the village owns a black rabbit".

"I don't know that", Akritas said as bluntly, eager to put an end to the animal's suffering, that suddenly reminded him of...

"Well, I know!" the priest replied. Then he laughed. "I'm their spiritual leader. Don't I know what kinds of rabbits they keep in their backyards?"

"If that's so..." Akritas replied, regretting his earlier tone. "However..."

Father Stavros took the animal from Rodi's hands and palpated it with the air of a connoisseur, estimating its weight.

"Well, well, it's quite plump!"

"Hold on, I think that..." Akritas began as he remembered that Maria had brought the rabbit with her a few minutes ago, when she returned from her walk.

The priest, either not hearing or deliberately ignoring Akritas' plea to stop what he was about to do, raised the small animal, weighed it with a quick once over and with the edge of his right palm hit it hard at the base of its neck. Then, he let it fall.

"... I would rather..." Akritas muttered belatedly.

"That's that!" said the priest and asked Rodi for a sharp knife.

"Did you just knock it out?" Akritas asked, perturbed, worried.

"Why did you…"

"Done!" the other man proudly responded.

After a few spasmodic tremors, the animal lay unmoving, stretched out on the floor. Father Stavros lifted it up, carved the fur with the knife, at the height of the neck, and shoving his fingers between skin and flesh, dexterously exposed its trunk in a single movement.

Like a fur coat on a naked female body, the animal's pelt slipped to the ground. A few arteries still pulsated, as guts and intestines hung loose bloating the belly that fell by the joints of the thighs.

"You're fantastic, Father Stavros!" Rodi felt obliged to remark, observing a gleam of pride in the eye of the clergyman.

Joseph felt sick to his stomach. The way…

Father Stavros grinned smugly and sank the knife into the ridiculous belly. Fingers deep in the stab wound, he pulled out the intestines, still steaming! Then, bringing the sharp kitchen knife to the root of the neck, he severed head from trunk.

"Give the guts to the dog", he commanded Rodi.

The young girl opened the door that led to the yard and called Roxy. The dog rushed to her. Without touching, it sniffed the red mass in front of it. Then, lifting its head, it exposed its teeth with a threatening growl before barking at the girl's face, teeth brushing against her neck. At the last minute she pulled back, neck sprinkled with drool. The dog then ran away panting, squeezing between the wire fence and the railing which cut at it till it bled, before it disappeared on the uphill road.

Hearing the commotion, Maria stepped into the kitchen.

"It's Roxy… He bit me, ma'am!" the girl complained, wiping eyes and nose with her bloody hands.

"Why?"

Before receiving a reply, Maria saw, out of the corner of her eye, the black fur wrapped offhandedly in a newspaper. The priest had asked for it, intending it for his stivali boots.

"What have you slain?"

"A wild rabbit", Father Stavros replied. "It came right on time!"

"It was wondering around in the yard", Joseph explained. "It made its way into the chicken shed…"

"It is said", the priest spoke again, "that rabbit's blood is excellent for ladies in your condition. Very nutritious indeed!"

Before he had time to finish his exaltation, Maria walked out of the room, pale, with sad eyes and trembling lips. She shut herself in the bedroom and burst into tears.

Joseph looked at the priest with powerless wrath, slammed the door that separated the corridor from the living room and the guests' voices, then tentatively walked to her door. He knocked; there was no answer. He called her name again and again, tried to open the door; to no avail. He went back to the kitchen.

"She's crying", he said. He had the air of someone lost.

"That's a good sign!" the clergyman assured him. "Nothing out of the ordinary for a pregnant woman. It was about time you found out yourself! Just be patient, you'll get the hang of it when the second baby arrives".

And he explained to Rodi how to salt and marinate the rabbit — "a skill that requires caution and dexterity!" He helped himself to a bit of sizzled liver and started chewing.

"Ambrosia!" he exclaimed.

Whilst looking at the priest absentmindedly, Joseph saw once

again, ever so clearly, the earthen edges of the immense collective grave, with the dried roots of ancient trees, in the clearing,
in Africa, amidst jackals and eagles crowing; or in Cyprus, with
the red-berets and their backup all around that receptacle of a
pile of maimed bodies.

Late in the afternoon, when she came back from the grocery
store, together with the groceries, Rodi brought her madam a
letter.

"I forgot to give it to you. It's from that foreign lady".

Maria took the letter eagerly and examined the plain white envelope. There was nothing written on it. She opened it.

> *"Dear Maria,*
>
> *Today we received the greatest news of our lives. Please allow us
> to call on you tomorrow, at 7:00 pm. Give our love to Mr Akritas.
> Piotr and Hanna".*

Rodi sorted out the groceries and, carrying under her arm the
bundle of dresses and knitwear that Maria had given her in the
morning, was getting ready to go home.

"Is there anything else you need, madam?"

"Yes, please, hold on a moment".

She went to the small room which served as the study, took a
piece of paper and a pen, and noted:

> *"Thank you. We'll be expecting you. We'll dine together. Maria".*

She folded the note and placed it in an envelope, the only one she found in Avgi's small desk. At the corner, their friends' name and village address was printed: 8, Kourdala str., Spilia. She licked it closed, then, on a second piece of paper, she made a list of supplies.

"This if for Ms Archangielsk. The list is for tomorrow".

"The greatest news of our lives". Had she not known how precise and frugal they were with words, she would have considered the phrase maliciously poetic or cornily polite, and think no more of it. But, of course, they were neither poets nor typically polite. Therefore, what they had written, they meant. Or was it an indirect way of letting her know that they too had found out what was by now common knowledge in the entire village – they, ignorant to the quirks of indirect discourse?

She found Joseph in the living room. He was leafing through his notes, arranging photographs and tapes from his trunk – those he had thrown back there, as if they were a swarm of wasps, on the night of the Archangielsks. He hadn't touched them since that Saturday.

"They're coming tomorrow", she told him. "The Archangielsks. I invited them for dinner".

He carried on, in silence, arranging the photographs according to the number on each, paring them with handwritten captions. He placed the bundle in the trunk, then raised his eyes.

"Very well", he told her. Then, "Do I have to attend?"

"Do as you please".

She sat in a rocking chair by the window overlooking the backyard. Her palms she tenderly placed upon her belly. On the wake of that victory, she had made peace with her illness and her defeats, his alienation, the silence that weighed down the house…

Then, a loud knock startled her; looking around, she saw nothing. Something stirred inside her; or not. It wasn't just that momentary flinch, low in her solar plexus. There it was, something brushing against the window. She couldn't make out what. Perhaps the clematis or a shutter that Rodi had forgotten to close. Or, perhaps not...

She sought refuge in her reverie and the serenity afforded by their obscure phrase. "The greatest news of our lives". Then the jabbing resumed, more persistently, reminding her...

She got up and walked to the window, heard pecking and ruffling. She opened the window pane. Together with the fine rain that had erupted all of a sudden and doused her, with the wind that billowed the curtains and wrapped them around her neck, a pigeon flew into the room; it was black, a white dot on its forehead and eyes the colour of clear mauve. Identical to...

She tried hard to close the window and went back to her seat. The pigeon paced comically, alternately leaning to either side, then perched between her slippers.

"Are you cold?"

In spite of her strong protests, the Archangielsks bowed and kissed her hand. In their posture she saw respect, the same respect, as she recalled, they felt for Michael too. And this, more than the hand-kissing itself, was puzzling and embarrassing. She considered it unfitting, irrational, something between irony and provocation. But, at the same time, she suspected the gesture was hiding something else, something that moved her, that she would treasure in order to secretly relish later, by herself.

As a gift, Hanna brought her an album with Bach's grossos. Piotr offered her a demijohn with wine he himself had produced.

"Worthy of Bach!" he said, smiling.

They courteously shook Joseph's hand.

"Our warmest congratulations", they told him.   ·

Joseph fought a violent negative reaction, trying to smother it; he couldn't. In the end, he phrased it as mildly as he could:

"Thank you, on behalf of Maria..."

"Luckily, the great things that come to those we love are not without gain for us too", Piotr said, neither paltering nor hesitating. "In fact, more often than not it is we who benefit the most".

The four of them walked to the living room. Maria thanked them again for their presents and, to show her gratification, put the album on the record player. She adjusted the volume. Bach's celestial, mathematical prolixity filled the room, imposing silence. Only the pine cones in the fireplace insisted on interrupting the cyan serenity with their short screeching sounds and eruptions. At the end of the first movement, silence was broken. Maria filled four glasses with wine from the demijohn she had just been offered.

"I'll have whiskey", Joseph dryly declared and put the wine glass to the side.

The Archangielsks raised their glasses.

"To fortification!" they said.

"To fortification!" Maria repeated, without realizing the exact meaning of the toast.

"To health!" Joseph unwillingly hissed.

They brought the glasses to their lips.

"It's... Really!..." Maria muttered, looking for the right word. "Like..."

"A distant uncle of my father entrusted me with the recipe. A proper Methuselah! He lived in the Caucasus. He died at a hundred and forty three", Piotr smiled. "Of course, I don't mean to say that the wine was the only secret of his longevity".

Maria turned to Joseph.

"You should try it".

"Later", he vaguely answered and refilled his glass with whiskey.

Bach's music became even more distant, it neared the boundaries of the soundless. It unfolded slowly, akin to an endless sky-blue spiral, with golden edges and an indeterminate depth of white contemplation, in a seascape of calm and love that neither words nor concepts could determine. Maria was again immersed in a daze, a daze that, only now did she realize, was similar to the one she had felt the other day when she had received their white roses. It wasn't just similar, it was identical and... She couldn't find the word.

She struggled to step out of the safety of her silence:

"And for the roses", she said. "Thank you! They... their aroma was so rare! Where did you find them?"

"I grow them", Hanna replied.

"At this time of year?"

"We've made our own green house; it's small, five by five. Your friend, Avgi, and Mr Demetriades helped us. The two of them also helped Piotr install the distiller. You should come and see for yourself".

"I would love to".

"You too!" Piotr invited Joseph.

"Thank you", the other man said, coldly.

"Andante!" Hanna named the new movement of the concert.

Rodi stepped inside and, looking at her toes as always, announced:

"Dinner's served".

"Good evening, Rodi", Hanna greeted her.

The young girl blushed and muttered something indiscernible.

The pendulum clock in the corridor sounded eight.

They drank wine and ate a slice of halloumi cheese each, home-made pasta and salad.

Knowing their preferences, Maria didn't even suggest they should try the rest of the dishes: Arabian meatballs, tahini salad, imam with finely chopped garlic. In fact, she herself opted to eat only what they ate; except for a bit of smoked ham she hardly touched. Out of the corner of his eye, Joseph cast secret looks at them, his plate untouched.

"Could it be that the other secret of your uncle's longevity was vegetarianism?"

"Not at all!" Piotr exclaimed. "On the contrary, my uncle loved to eat meat. He had flocks of sheep and goats, therefore meat, either fresh or salted, was never absent from his table".

"I can't see why you are so moved by this topic", Maria phrased her accusation with a smile.

Rodi served a variety of cheeses, liqueur and French cognac, arranged on a wooden tray.

"I'd rather combine the cheese with some more of Mr Archangielsk's wine", Maria said. "Would you like to taste it now?" she asked Joseph.

"A drop!" he reluctantly said.

"Please bring the demijohn", she asked Rodi.

Joseph served the wine, pouring just a bit for himself. Before they raised it to their lips, Piotr stood up:

"Am I allowed a toast?" he asked. They all went silent and fixed their eyes upon him. "To the most beautiful thing that has ever occurred in our lives! It is safe to say that, Hanna, isn't it?"

And he looked at his wife, smiling. She responded positively: "It is".

"To the most beautiful thing that has ever occurred in my unbeautiful life", Maria raised her glass.

Joseph turned to Piotr in a provocative mood.

"What do you mean?" he snapped. "What is the most beautiful thing that has ever happened in your life?"

"The child! Maria's!"

Hearing her name, for the first time, from Piort's lips, she felt the same shiver she had felt when Michael first spoke to her. And something else, somewhat different; it was as if she had never before heard these sounds, as if the three familiar syllables suddenly took on a new meaning.

"And why, might I ask, is my wife's child the most beautiful occurrence of your life?" Joseph asked again. He stood up and pushed the chair behind him.

"Joseph!" Maria muttered.

"Because it's Mikael's too!" Piotr calmly replied.

Joseph remained speechless for a few moments, his face given to an icy expression. Then, he placed the glass of wine on the table, without tasting it, and walked briskly out of the room. No one moved. From the corridor they could hear his steps. He paused in front of the portmanteau.

"To fortification", Piotr raised his glass.

"To fortification", Hanna responded.

They both emptied their glasses.

Maria stared into the void. She didn't bring the wine to her lips, nor did she respond to the inexplicable toast.

The front door closed.

"What is he to you?" she asked, almost violently, when they took their seats again.

"A visitor! From the isles of light!" Hanna said.

"The father of your child", Piotr added. "Soon you will be able to grasp the meaning of this!"

"I can feel..." she answered as if reverberating. "I can feel it".

"May it be so! For the others too!"

"I wish Joseph could understand..."

How did they talk? How did she talk? Who? Why? How did

thoughts and their signifiers unfold and converge? And why did he leave? At this hour, this formal hour? Why was it formal? What was wrong with her?

Her eyes sank into his untouched wine.

"He'll understand", Piotr pursued her meditation. "When He arrives, your child. The others always benefit the most, those we love".

"But will he be born?"

"He will!"

"What about me?" she asked, staring into his eyes.

"You'll deliver the child".

"It all feels like a dream. Everything's happening and progressing along a chain of inexplicable coincidences: you, Avgi leaving on the day of our arrival, Michael coming to you, for me, Joseph's depression, my illness..."

"There are no coincidences, Maria, just laws. And your child is a gift from the most relentless ones, the same laws that will protect it".

"You speak a language I want to believe but cannot understand; if I could understand it, I would believe".

"Faith is useless; knowledge and love is all we need. If you try, you will reach both".

"How?"

"By bearing your child, our child".

"There's nothing I want more. Even if it's the last thing I'm... But it's not up to me".

"Up to you; up to your will to bring it to the world".

"Then it shall be born. This much I can promise, even if I lack knowledge".

They went from the dining room back to the living room. There, they sat comfortably in a triangular formation, Maria at the crest.

"Yes, I have made up my mind, I'll work with you; as long as you think I can make it".

"When do you start?" the Arckangielsks voiced their satisfaction.

"Whenever you're ready", Maria responded.

"We are, have been for a while now", he smiled, "we're just wait-ing for you", she completed his phrase as she always did.

"In my entire life, I have never worked, systematically, I mean".

"You can do much more than what we'll ask of you", he said, now in a more familiar tone.

"Besides, you've proven it", she smiled.

"How? When did I prove it?"

But they both fell silent, successively looking at one another, all three of them, then one of them at the other two, like three be-ginners, three novices, either lovers or conspirators. Until, sud-denly, he smiled; the two women laughed with him, aloud.

And the lump in Maria's throat immediately went away.

"Coffee, maybe?" she asked when they fell back into silence, faces calm.

"Only wine after my wine", he said.

"Only wine after his wine", she smiled, in a merry mood she hadn't discarded as crudely as he had.

"I've been meaning to ask, how do you make this nectar? What are the ingredients?"

"Graves juice, blossom flour and fermentation with ultra-violet and a few cosmic ones", Piotr replied, oscillating between serious and funny.

"What kind of blossoms?"

"It's a special hybrid of daisies".

"But…"

"A rare variety".

"I would like to see these daisies. And the place the wine is bottled…"

"By all means. But I do warn you, the place is not as interesting as the product itself".

"This is usually… in fact, always, the case, isn't it? Take me for instance".

"If it's any consolation, I assure you this is a universal law!"

"Radiation for minerals".

"Wine and colour and aroma for plants".

"Man and his music for animals".

"And for the few, the very few and humble privileged ones, a labour like yours, once every two millennia".

"Like mine?"

"Like yours".

"But… it's….You can't mean that".

"We have never said a word we didn't mean, Maria".

"A word that's not inferior to what we mean".

"Why am I privileged?"

"And indeed with a privilege you have earned! Both you and Joseph! He's not impartial to either your good and bad fortune. From now on, nothing will be given to you for free. This is the law! What you now have and what you will earn, you have gained through struggle and sacrifice, past and future alike".

"Sacrifice?"

"Privileges are but the products of sacrifice!"

The black Cadillac stopped in front of the "Lovely Spilia". The driver's window was wound down; through the gap emerged the chauffer's cap and half his head.

"The house of Joseph Akritas?"

"Past the church at 8, Kourdala str., the new house", Nicodemus answered and curiously fixed his gaze on the passenger in the back seat.

He was smoking a cigar, indifferent to their conversation and the curiosity it provoked. He was elegant, unyielding and distant.

"Thank you", said the chauffer and drove on cautiously, calculating both width and distance; the street could barely accommodate his thirty wild horses.

"Who was that gentleman?" Demetriades asked. "I'm sure I've seen him before".

"He's either a judge or a lawyer; or a doctor. I've seen him too, on TV. Perhaps he's an ambassador; yes, an ambassador!" said the Community President.

"There's no doubt you know who he is, mukhtar", the sergeant spoke in innocent irony.

"It's him!" Father Stavros assured himself once his connotations verified his memory. "Mr Serghides! Of 'Serghides and Fardis'. Big shot lawyers!"

"See I was right?" bragged the Community President. "I knew I'd seen him somewhere".

"Whiskey on the rocks, please".

"Rodi! Bring ice and savouries".

Joseph walked to the buffet, to serve the drinks.

"I'm sorry Ms Akritas is not in", Serghides feigned to care. "We haven't seen each other in months".

"She comes back after six. Perhaps if you could stay for dinner. It would give us great pleasure".

"Impossible!" the other man rejected the invitation. "I have an urgent appointment with an Arab, rich as Croesus. He's about to make a multi-million investment, you see! He's not the kind of man you would leave waiting. Quite simply, they never wait".

Joseph offered him the drink and sat down.

"Well?" Serghides said with a smile, expecting an answer to a question he hadn't asked, but was certain troubled his interlocutor.

"No", Akritas gave a firm reply.

And just like that, without any introduction or beating around the bush, the discussion that had begun weeks ago through phone calls, telegraphs and teletext, resumed; only to reassert the denial Akritas had declared during their first meeting, sometime after his return to Cyprus.

"The deadline we have given you has already expired", Serghides said, mildly, and raised the crystal glass to his lips.

"..."

"Cheers! Here's to me changing your mind".

"..."

They both drank.

"I'm sure you know that in case you insist there will be consequences. You'll leave us no other choice but to seek recourse in action against you. And I'm afraid that the decisions I have set forth in my letter will be far more unpleasant once materialized than as a friendly warning".

"Do you consider your last letter a friendly one?"

"Given the gravity of the case in question, I most certainly do! I must confide that your case was one of the very few where I had allowed my amical interest to alleviate the rigidity of the law".

"Am I to assume that what you just said provides the measure of your determination?" Akritas said, miming the lawyer's tone and phraseology.

"Precisely! And I'm happy you're getting the message. Not that I had any doubts about it. You know how much I appreciate you and the manner in which I have always promoted your best interests".

"Where are you getting at?" Akritas said, now annoyed by Serghides' hypocritical noblesse.

"To the extent you are right, you may see in me a friend; now, where you are wrong..."

"I've no doubt that in the case at hand you are convinced I am wrong", Akritas said and finished his drink.

"I'm afraid that facts and numbers condemn you".

He too finished his drink, placed the glass on the coffee table and opened his briefcase. From there he took a bundle of original documents and photocopies.

"My arsenal. All the evidence!" he said.

"Don't bother. I won't question any of it!"

But Serghides ignored the appeal.

"All things must be done in order!" he said. "On the 26th of December, on the Agency's instructions, you left for South Africa, Lagos, Biafra, Rhodesia. As usual, you had been provided with an open-ended ticket, a check book for accommodation and representation expenses, blank; a written statement for full coverage of any unanticipated expenses pertaining to your work, as well as the standard margin for undeclared costs: for gratuities, purchase of information, "tips" and so on and so forth. From Africa you flew first class to the Middle East, then Kashmir and Indochina, a week in Jakarta. I have been informed that, during the span of this particular period, you have accumulated material which, judging from your earlier work and habitual performance, translates into money and prestige for the Agency, making up a noteworthy investment. However, not even one good report or newsreel do you deliver for this entire period... Sometimes you return to your base, in fact prematurely. Justifiably, the Agency heads expect an explanation. And you, by way of an answer, declare you have no intention of delivering your material. They, because they are so appreciative of your work, and make special arrangements for your sake, offer a reasonable deadline. Upon my personal intervention and pressures, this deadline is extended, until it expires without you having offered any text or film, even though you yourself admitted to the chief editor who came specifically from London to see you, that the material is there. Again following my interventions, instead of taking legal action against you, we offer you a twenty-day leave of absence, in the hope that rest and relaxation will help you think more calmly; again, to no avail. So please tell me, what's left for us to do?"

"This is your problem".

"And yours too. Mainly yours! I am not aware of your financial situation; whichever it may be, the twenty-two thousand you will be obliged to pay is not insignificant for anyone... The eight thousand correspond to your travel expenses and the worth of a mini-camera that has been destroyed whilst in your possession. The rest of the money represents your providence fund, which will be withheld according to your employment contract, insurances, hidden expenses and, of course, personal expenses! Please note that as of this month and until final settlement of this issue, your monthly salary and other benefits will be set aside".

He neatly arranged the papers on the briefcase and smiled:

"And I repeat the classic question: So?"

Joseph Akritas was looking at him in silence.

"Do try, dearest Joseph, to act in your own best interest. Or, to put it more discreetly, not to act against your own good. How much will you lose by adopting barren denial? Needless to say that, once the case becomes widely known, you will lose something else too, even more valuable: you are pulverizing your career; you will be forever excluded from journalism".

"Quite often, of late, I wonder if, in order to achieve this deposition, I should indeed pay the price", Akritas replied and stood up.

"Well! That's just..." the other man sneered.

"What? What is it?" Akritas raised his tone, annoyed. "What do you know of journalism, my dear Serghides, aside from the fixed profit it offers you?"

"Never mind what journalism is for me, dear Joseph. What I know is that, until recently, for you it was the quintessence of your life".

"Yes, of course. Because I was looking at it through a distorted glass, because I was an idealist, a utopian, thinking I was serving a sacred cause, delivering the X-rays that exposed the carcinomas of our age, our society, facilitating the performance of surgery, facilitating catharsis! That's all. And if you ask any decent, if blinkered, colleague of mine, he'll tell you the same thing. Self-persuasion. Until they finally discover, just as I have, that we're chasing a chimera. Or even worse; we're the only ones who do care and the only ones who can't see reality for what it is. The truth is, our contemporary readers and viewers can only be moved by carcinomas, theirs and the others', which they assimilate; by easy success and money, which they don't assimilate. Nothing else will move them, that's the measure, the sense of their lives. No one has ever cared enough to sever them; much less those who could have. And at the end of the day, all of us who are feeding the Moloch of the Media, the only thing we really achieve is a strengthening of the disease. By dissecting it and adding all sorts of macabre details and all the familiar, horrible symptoms, we allow it to spread and metastasize, to flare up. There has not been a single case of annoying truth I have brought to the light where my contribution has led to the changes I was anticipating. I have only witnessed the hypocritical declarations of the guilty ones and the crocodile tears of the masses. No one has ever been unbestialized in the face of extreme danger. No one has ever dropped the gun or turned it where he should have".

"Assuming this is how things are, just like you're describing them, what can you do? You or anyone else? There is no way we can change overnight a situation that is, by your own admission, global".

"I know; I have tried it. That's why I've ended up in Spilia".

"And this is your right, of course, even though I could juxtapose a series of arguments suggesting the opposite. It's not enough for us to put our hands up and quit, exorcising hope with our defeat. This kind of attitude had been both expressed and exhausted during Gandhi's lifetime. His own disciples never really adhered to it. If we have the guts, let's turn our weapons against those responsible – and I don't mean tangible weapons, though sometimes it does appear... Anyway, in this particular case, by weapons I mean your pen, your lens. You can't say they haven't produced some positive results. Granted, they haven't put an end to any local or other war... perhaps none of your reports or films has led to specific measures – though they might at some point. But I do believe you have awakened the consciousness of several. And it is these changes that weigh the most... albeit in the long term!"

He was silent for a while, then relit the cigar that had been put out and carried on behind a cloud of smoke:

"There's something I'd like to suggest, though I do realize your decision is final; in any case, it won't change in the near future, right? However, before you decide on what to do from now on, as – at least this is what I believe – you have no intention of becoming either a poet or an anchorite, don't you think you should first fulfil the obligations you have taken on? Wouldn't this be more honourable and less painful both for you and everyone else? Deliver the material you withhold; allow it to be published and then... then you can revise. Of course, as you know, it is too late for the Agency to circulate footage and news pertaining to past events; however, I pledge to contribute towards another formula, agreed between you and me, that will satisfy both sides. We could, for instance, present your material in the form of a book or a documentary; or a Black Bible. What do you say?"

"..."

"Well?"

"I'll have to think about it".

"Please do!" the other man replied, attempting to hide his satisfaction behind a puff of smoke. "At the same time, you do understand that this mustn't take too long. Time is of the essence".

"I will get back to you; soon, I hope".

Her work with the Archangielsks she had envisioned and desired differently; a diaconate devoid of sentimental breaks and parentheses, a spiritual overstimulation combined with experiences which, as the days passed, would expand her horizons and solve the troubles that plagued her.

"To be honest", she confessed to Hanna Archangielsk, one week after she had begun working with them, "I'm a bit disappointed. I was hoping this engagement would help me forget".

"Nothing in the world can help you do that", was the answer she was given. "The secret for every cure is to nurture hope alongside fear; alongside panic, be able to see victory waiting in the corner".

"What kind of victory can I expect?"

"His nativity!"

"Even this has been reduced to a nightmare. What will he become of if he survives labour? I already feel guilty. I've betrayed
my child before I've had the chance to love it..."

"When it's time you'll realize how groundless your fears are".

"I wish it be so! But I'm afraid to put so many... in fact all my
hopes into this single gift".

"Is there anything bigger than this?"

There was a long pause. They both went back to their work,
Hanna painstakingly drawing in her "Sketchbook" every new sec-
tor of the wall-painting that was revealed by their surgical work;
Maria describing the scenes thoroughly, dryly, in her "Record
Book".

"Shepherd, on his knees, headless; nothing suggests the painter
had made it, painted it, that the artist had painted it; and not on
his knees, perhaps kneeling or bent on one knee; and someone later
removed or erased it; workman with the tools of his trade, the tools
of the construction worker or of the builder or just craftsman with
the tools of his craft, no neck or mouth; jaw sunk into the chest;
deep into the chest. No; just into the chest. Ears big, conical, like
an animal's. A magus with a precious crown, just crown, without
the adjective, no diadem or porphyry attire; here, the adjective
serves as noun; better say, just porphyry. The mantle is open and
drawn on either side of the chest, or on the chest which is gaping,
as if a huge bullet had pierced it through and through. Is "huge"
necessary? It is; it's..."

"When I first met you, before you suggested I worked with you",

Maria pursued her earlier line of thought, "I was anticipating... help from you. A transfusion of your faith".

"Faith in what, Maria?"

"In... in immortality. In man's survival. In everything that's un-related to premature death. And everything..."

"We have no faith to pass on, Maria. It's been a long time since the Archangielsks put faith aside. Now we serve and believe in what we love".

"What do you love? This is what I want to know. This is what I should've asked you in the first place".

"What we love and know cannot be handed down. Not because we are enviously guarding it, but because you run the risk of believing it before you actually love it, of wanting it before you redeem it. And that's a sad substitute, beneath the mother of your child".

"I don't understand you. I believe... no, I know this for a fact! – death and the void, my irrationality and fears, to you they... you've overcome them. So why isn't it possible for you to be-queath your faith and knowledge to me? To help me out of this terrible..."

"There's knowledge that can be offered and knowledge that can be conquered. What you're asking falls within the category of the things that cannot be offered for free. You need to fight, bleed, subdue the beast within you in order to earn what you seek".

"When? I don't have much time left".

"You've got as much time as needed".

"What does that even mean?" she smiled bitterly, now calmer and more composed. "Is it a transfusion of knowledge or hope?"

"It's a law".

Piotr Archangielsk climbed down the scaffold. It was time to rest for a few minutes; he took a glance at Hanna's drawings and Maria's notes.

"Well, the famous Panselinos himself would gladly sign your drawings!" he told Hanna with a smile, then leant over Maria's handwritten notes: "How are we progressing?"

"I'm doing my best".

"Carry on then!" he addressed both of them.

With Hanna he walked to the narthex where, on a chair and on the ground around it, they kept all their paraphernalia: the tools of their trade, a bag of supplies and a portable closet for the raincoats, the rubber boots, gloves, and the blouses they had on while working. And as he did every day since their collaboration had first begun, Piotr came back with a goblet of wine. "So early in the morning?" she had asked him on the first day. "For some varieties of wine it's never too early and never too late". The time she had spent with them had proved him right; now she couldn't imagine the first break of the day without a glass of the red semi-dry wine she would slowly sip, by taking small mouthfuls, supplementing each with an apple or a pear; it was as unthinkable for her to eat anything other than herbs and dried nuts or not to walk for five or six kilometres a day, regardless of the weather. They told her she could either walk with them to the chapel or drive there on her own; she had opted to walk. On the first few days she occasionally felt bouts of tiredness, hypoglycaemia, hunger. Within two or three weeks she got over it. In fact so much had she gotten used to this pace and exercise, that the entire route seemed to her like a piece of cake, even though it was "really hard work for a lady in your condition", as the priest had suggested one day they had met on the road. "It's true, sometimes I do feel a bit tired, but I don't mind it!" she replied, on a different occasion, to a similar insinuation by Joseph. "It relaxes muscles and nerves. I've always had trouble sleeping; now I fall asleep as soon as I lie down… Besides, the doctor, rather the council of doctors, when they saw me the other day, unanimously agreed that "physical exercise is beneficial". After all, if at some point I feel less vibrant, I can drive the Deux Chevaux". – "Father Stavros says they've imposed various habits on you" – "Father Stavros does not know. Even though I would have very much liked to imitate them in so many ways, I even asked permission to do so, they said no. As if that very denial was the cornerstone of their philosophy". – "What about intellectual work? Don't you find it exhaustive?" Joseph asked in that rare demonstration of interest. "At first, yes, I thought it was boring; and pointless. But never exhaustive like the way you put it. I was afraid it would dry me out, that I would find it boring to describe what I see, to the slightest detail, without offering my own judgement or interpretation, without adjectives or thoughts. Nothing of my own. Become a soulless camera, like the ones you own. There were moments, I do admit, when this practice of plain, utter precision made me restless. But I overcame it, without actually realizing when or how. It was done at a moment I don't recall… Now I'm interested in it, I like it, working relaxes my thoughts and emotions. At times, when I write about the sinner's dislocated arm and the biblical Joseph's concerned gaze, without seeking to determine why he's concerned, avoiding even the slightest assumption on what has caused it, when I essentialize the very few adjectives I'm allowed to use, by denuding words and ideas, I feel as if I'm taking a cold bath. I'm appeased. These two parallel exercises, walking and this, help me forget who I am, what's in store for me – and that's a blessing!" – "If this is truly the case, I have no objection…" – "But even if it hadn't been so, your objection wouldn't have mattered at all…" – "Why do you say that, Maria? You never talked this way before…" – "Yes, never. In fact now, there are times when I think that you and I never really talked as we do now, so substantially".

Their break was over. She had a slice of apple that had been left over and grabbed hold of her pen and exercise book. Hanna took the marker, the crayons and the Sketchbook.

"Piotr estimates that by your delivery date the wall-painting will have been restored", she told her.

"It seems to me everything will be over on that day".

"Or everything will begin", Piotr offered with a smile.

He kindly asked them to plug in the spotlight projector. It was cloudy outside, light was sparse. The projector sliced through the twilight and highlighted a fraction of the work:

> "*Two overaged angels or archangels, with white hair and beard and feminine or womanly breasts, or just breasts, breasts loose on the bare bosom, holding an inscription: "liberation". There's no other word, as if everything else has been deliberately erased by the artist's brush*".

She reread the phrase and deleted the words *deliberately* and *brush,* as well as the insinuating phrasing *as if.* And she made the necessary corrections. All that was left was:

> "*There's no other word; everything else has been erased by the icon-painter*".

He was looking at her through the window, hidden behind the curtains in the living room. Aside from the dog, now she had to look after the three birds she had tamed and put up in the covered area of the yard, making nests and separate provisions for each: the pigeon, the sparrow, the goldfinch. They would eat spores from the palm of her hand, tweet upon seeing her emerging from the house, flutter about her or sit on her shoulder or head.

"Santa Francesca of the Caves of Spilia!"

He went back to his study and sat in front of the notepaper: *Dear Mr Serghides.* A bare address, with neither the possibility nor the will to continue. He imagined himself going out into the yard, approaching her: "They've presented me with the following dilemma; to either compromise or face their trampling of me! And I have to answer. Do I?" – "What is it you really want? This is what you should do". – "You're feeding them from the palm of your hand, even the cowardly goldfinch. It's because you're... They feel safe near you, just as I have felt so far, though I hid it; out of egotism and rage. Honestly, Maria, I don't feel humiliated by what has happened, not at all! You are free to either stay or go, with him or alone. I will not deprive you of this right which, in any case, I lack. I will not deprive you of my love – if that means something to you. My frolics were the masks of my powerless love, of envy. I will not go back to that, I swear! What I really want now is for you to fight this illness and vanquish it. I want you to live and bear our child! I love it because it will come out of you, it will pain you! Promise me this!" And she would turn with tears in her eyes and say: "That's all there is, Joseph, my child!" – "Is it really there?" – "Yes, it is".

He crumpled the notepaper with the address and stepped outside into the yard. As he approached, the birds flew back to their nests, the dog walked away.

"Have I interrupted something?" he asked.

"No, they're full".

There was a pause. Then:

"I've been watching you", he told her. "And I came to let you know…"

"What?"

He needed to drive back to the city on account of serious obligations. He would be away for two or three days. Perhaps more. If she needed the car, he could leave it. He could drive back with Lefteris.

"I don't need it".

"What if you do?"

"I've never needed it upon discovering my legs".

"Very well! I hope to be back before your next check-up".

"No rush, I won't go back to the city unless it's time…"

"Why this denial?" he asked with a sudden interest. "I realize that Dr Herodotou wants to see you quite often".

"It's pointless. I've been hearing the same things over and over again, for months now. Of course, I suppose it's good that it doesn't change. But now I've got other priorities aside from my cancer. I've got my work. I can't be away at "Hygeia" for a whole day without good reason".

"You stand to gain more than losing a day".

"I'll decide that, Joseph".

"Yes you will, Maria. But do allow me to note something – though as you said I don't have the right. What you're doing with the two foreigners is the most pointless, vain work I've ever heard of. It's work without meaning. Unless it's just a pretext they're using to keep you close to them all the time".

"You've a right to believe whatever suits you the most. As for me, I'm at an age when I can decide for myself what I must or mustn't do".

"Since the day those two appeared in our lives, our worlds have come tumbling down".

"They're not responsible for it! And if now you talk the way you do, it's not because you're interested in my health or the conditions of my work, it's only because I've tried to find what you had lost, what you hadn't been unable to offer me!"

"That's not fair; and you know why".

"I don't know Joseph; neither do I care".

Silence fell for a while. Then, even though he had decided not to talk to her yet of what he had exchanged with Serghides, her reaction aggravated him and he felt the need to bring her back to reality, and cruelly so.

"I guess you're right, you don't know why. Still, you should care as much as I do. I've been keeping this from you, but I'd rather you knew about it instead of misrepresenting myself. So, in brief: I'm obliged to pay the Agency twenty two thousand Cyprus pounds", he began, trying to keep his calm and impartiality, though not too consciously. "To make amends! Or, I should agree to their terms".

He lit his pipe, waiting for her reaction, a comment, an indication she understood the totality of the problem that was hers too. Then, certain that his preface hadn't impressed her, he employed more dramatic details: "I'm afraid I have to sell off the house in Nicosia, the collections too, our porcelains and paintings; and perhaps the garden, to offer it as a plot of land".

"If you do decide to cut yourself away, don't hesitate on my behalf! I'll be the first to cheer for you!"

"Do you really mean that?" he asked with disappointment blended with relief. "You have no objection? For the house, our paintings, the garden?"

"Of course I mean that. As for the house, pretty soon I will personally have no use for it".

"What about the child? Where do you intend... your child to live?"

"I don't know. I hope he'll live a free man like his father".

Her reply incited him anew. She was unfair to him, contentious. And to think he was ready to open his heart to her! He was urged to strike back without hesitation:

"Who will take care of it?" he asked and fixed his gaze upon her. "Even Christ and the Buddha had to be nurtured for a while! Someone had to change their diapers! This is what I'm talking about. What will become of the child if... the undesirable were to happen. I think you'd prefer I was direct with you".

"Of course. And you do it so eagerly. I don't know. I suppose it will no longer be my problem".

He realized he had crossed the boundaries; what he had asked for with his lips and eyes, he didn't mean. It would be unmanly to yield to her provocations.

"You speak with frivolous certainty", he told her. "You don't know, nor can your doctors make a safe prediction. I spoke to them too. They're optimistic. Perhaps your new friends..."

"Are the only ones who don't guess".

"What do they say?"

"That we live only for as long as we need to. We don't depart before we learn what we have to".

"What about us? What's still there for us to learn, Maria?"

"Perhaps a lot!"

"Perhaps nothing!"

"If this is what you believe, then according to their way of thinking, you're already dead. But do allow me..."

"Oh yes, I've known I'm dead for some time now. I know it, I've
said it time and again. But not according to their viewpoint; according to mine. And this, my dear, weighs heavier still".

"No! If it were so, you wouldn't... the way you react about the
Agency's issue. You're still fighting".

"I'm not fighting, Maria. I'm struggling to death".

Driving the Deux Cheavaux outside the "Lovely Spilia", he saw
Demetriades standing under the arch of the veranda, waving at
him to stop; he ignored him, raised his hand vaguely and drove
on.

Further down, at the bend before the uphill road, he almost
grazed against old woman Cleonice who was walking back from
her orchard carrying firewood. With a sudden manoeuver he
turned the wheel to avoid her at the risk of crashing into the
stone wall. He stepped on the brakes. His head jarred against
the window, but he wasn't hurt. He turned back to make sure
he hadn't nipped her. Always looking ahead, the old woman
trudged on in muddy waters, unaware of the peril she had nar-
rowly avoided.

He drove on, enmeshed in a fog that, as he continued on the
Karvounas-Troodos main road, fell and became all the more
thick, almost impenetrable. He had to cut speed over and again,

reducing to ten to fifteen kilometres per hour, the wipers working in vain, the headlights projecting a triangle in front of the car, barely measuring three by three metres.

Still, he carried on – though "dead", but according to his own viewpoint, not hers. "You're reacting", she had told him a few days ago, he can't remember on what occasion; "and you're fighting". Perhaps she was right! It wasn't an easy decision, but he had taken it. Had he indeed? If he had truly decided, wouldn't he have already contacted Serghides? So, no, he hadn't really decided. He's still struggling with death.

"As for me, I… I want to learn. I don't believe…"

This is what she'd told him, word for word. And if she still wants to learn… It seems that the ailments of the body are less detrimental than the ailments of our thymus. "I don't believe". And, according to the axiom of her mentors, for as long as she doesn't acquiesce, she will live on and rise above and… And more than that. Her envious self-restraint, the peacefulness of the spirit, whether genuine or apparent, he didn't know, the strength she drew… where from? Her resilience and patience, now, in her condition, when every cell was subject to exhaustive trials! She'd been working for twelve, fourteen hours per day! For weeks now. A few months ago, when she was still well, if something like that was to happen, for instance when they'd have guests over or if she'd decide to read a book non-stop or help him type his notes, she'd be overcome by migraines, complain about aches in her back, her hands, her kidneys.

There was no doubt about it, regardless of what he accused them of, they had subjected her to a very effective treatment.

Perhaps, why not? He could imitate her. It wouldn't be the first time! She was always one step ahead! But even if he made up his mind, he wouldn't ask anyone for help. He could, on his own, convert infidelity and denial into strength, impose a new pace on himself, a schedule for 'rising from the dead'. He could be the sole witness of success or of the more likely...

But even if he were to secretly implement some form of self-suggestion, which one would he choose? How would he progress? Never in the past had he been able to devote himself, in both soul and body, to anything unless it had already become his experience and passion.

On the other hand, the kind of work that had benefitted her so much was completely irrelevant to her interests, something that had never occurred to him to try.

Could it be that yielding to a contradictory situation was the secret of success? Why doesn't he try it? Take an axe and start chopping wood? Build a wall in the yard; weave a basket or write a rhymed poem, ten thousand verses long, about Spilia. Or... Why not? Serghides had offered him this choice: juxtapose the white against the black in a black and white Bible. Then again, why should it be black and white for the Agency and not white for himself?

No, no... That wasn't his aim, a new exhaustive engagement. What he sought for was stupor, a daze, forgetting the carcinoma in his mental mind, isolating it!

"I wish it were possible! But it isn't".

When he reached Troodos square and stepped into the only café he found open, the few guests looked at him in awe of his courage to travel on such a night! On the radio they said that all roads to Olympus were inaccessible and the fog was pierced by lightning and murderous flashes.

She heard the rail squeaking and the engine dying with a tremor. His feet wallowed in the muddy yard. From the wide open window, music left the house. The almond tree cast a blossomed branch in front of the window and the landscape gained back its range of colours: from grey to green, silver, gold, red, cyan.

The music depicted the sky while she was relishing the earth.

"Shall I bring you a quick bite, madam?"

"No, thank you Rodi".

"But madam…"

"Alright, bring something!"

Rodi came back with a tray. Wine and a side plate with a few slices of *flaouna*.

"Goodnight, madam".

Rodi left. He left too. Rodi to work at a mountainous trout fishery. He, just like he did every night, would either walk in order to get tired or have a cognac at the "Lovely Spilia". Easter had come and gone, May would be almost over, so quickly that it overwhelmed them. What would Easter have been if she hadn't visited them? *Tsourekia* and red eggs, lamb on the spit, egg-and-lemon soup, in the early hours of dawn, after Doxology, and a wish so overused that it had been drained of its profound meaning, one that could never be verified.

She went there with half a dozen red eggs and two *tsourekia*. She found them reading, a book for her, a newspaper for him. "Christ has risen", she uttered her wish.

They shook her hand, then freed a chair from a pile of books and pushed it towards her. She took a seat. Then, instead of the usual wish he had heard others utter, Piotr replied:

"For Jesus. From Jesus".

Nothing else. No other reference to the significance of the day.

They spoke of their work at the chapel, the temperature that had begun to rise and change the landscape, the decision of the Community Council to erect a hotel or hostels to attract tourists — and the like. But that unique phrase with the ambiguous meaning had been deposited upon her soul, magnetizing her thoughts, demystifying theirs. She didn't ask what they meant. Even if she had asked, she knew she wouldn't have received a reply. It was enough that it had been said, and she knew it had been uttered only for her; this hadn't occurred by chance, nor had the other thing that Hanna said as if in passing: *that it's pointless for Christmas and the Resurrection to be celebrated on the same date for everyone. There's a secret date for every human being; otherwise religion is reduced to a custom.* Those dispersed thoughts had awakened something within her but she didn't try to assign a meaning to them, neither at that particular moment nor later. Perhaps she was afraid she couldn't do it; or maybe she sensed the answer she would eventually deliver herself in the near future.

She took a slice of *flaouna*. The salty taste of cheese combined with the raisins made her feel sick. She bent over and clenched her stomach between sternum and knees, to keep herself from vomiting. And the foetus squirmed! Yes! For the first time ever his life stood apart from hers! Heart racing, her eyes welled up with tears.

"It's alive! It's alive in its grave! It's alive! You're alive God! I'm alive, I am!"

Thus she made sure her own Easter was on its way.

In three months, sometime between mid-August and 15 September. A Leo or a Virgo!

What had started to exacerbate his eagerness and concern, and this to an extent that was unnaturally fast and pressing, was the realization that the incidents he could record in the "White Bible" he had feverously begun writing, were far more than what he had initially estimated, so much so that he had to scrutinize everything.

A fog of forgotten incidents in war fields, riots, demonstrations, bloody conflicts, rapes, decapitations, emerged and became intertwined , first rigidly and vaguely, then with the blinding lucidity of a bolt of lightning, with boldness and clarity and geometrical multiplication. They were paralyzing, undermining the foundations of his worldview, altering his basic conclusions for the Communication Media, the stereotypical forms he had gradually crystalized. They were giving rise to this concern – could it be that what he had set out to do after his initial evaluation and recording was yet another expression of unjustified offhandedness?

Words, either worn or whole, casually cast into sentences; gestures and expressions and motions, perilous decisions of the earth's Powerful, hovering for a while before disappearing into the abominable void, but also actions of overwhelming humanity, heroic altruism and sacrifice, on the smallest scales, at decision-making centres or across the deserts of tribulation and hunger.

Insignificant incidents, tossed into the omnivorous funnel. Seconds of breathing amidst the great asthma. Fractions of a second of self-denial or ingenious sadism within the iron-barred cannibals he had captured and photographed and perpetuated in films, reports, into matter for contemplation. Everywhere. Almost everywhere and always. Present yet debased; not tradable; not lucrative. Little songbirds escaping a burning forest, their voice swallowed by the roaring of big animals at death's door.

They're almost shapeless; stories without specific diagrams. Kindness has no clear form, no perspective; it has neither a present nor a future. Just as nobility and death have no specific history, though death be the ultimate nobility, the ultimate great history, the magnificent black that absorbs and hoards clandestinely and potentially all colours. And it's beautiful. It's the ultimate recreation; and the ultimate extension; the exultant moral to the story. Yes, now that he was recording the minute details of the plus, he started to suspect how big a plus the greatest minus was, the ultimate pain. The transition from numerous pains and few pleasures to the unperturbed, the perennial, the dissolution of then and tomorrow, of the past century and the future one, evermore...

Oh, the redemption and peace! What a blessing for the starving, choleric, bleeding, reeking, disconcerted humanity!

How could he not have seen it in so many years? How could he not have suspected it? How did he wander, anxious, soiling the negatives of film and his soul with grimaces, the pain and the hatred and the other aspect of things, without seeing, suspecting the only eternity of man? The greatness of the soul that withdraws?

But no! What was he writing? The grand vicious circle! A rondo! Again and again he would reach the same ending, the same finish from a different route. Or was he just reversing the elements of the equation and instead of calculating the result by subtraction was doing so by addition? Was he struggling to employ alchemy, alien to our time and to his character, in order to equate the greater evil with the minimum good? Or was he degrading himself into a litterateur?

Whatever he was doing, nevertheless, he felt that something inside him had begun; a kind of fermentation. Work therapy or self-suggestion or whatever else one might call it, the great stupefaction even, had started to galvanize his soul. They had found just a tiny way out and they were secretly extending it, widening it, fumbling with nails, teeth and feet. Where and when would they lead him out into a clearing?

Where would Maria be led with work therapy and self-suggestion? Where did the Archangielsks intend to guide her? To the final destination from a road less painful?

What was he really looking for? Perhaps to reach his own grave with less sorrow… And this expectation, this aim, he was afraid to confess, afraid to enjoy, though he had already begun nearing them, yes he had…

At night, for three weeks now, a month, almost two, he can't remember for how long, he would sit hermetic opposite her, sharing only the essential, working and expanding the experiment, to suffocate, to delete 'the great volumes of depravity he had captured in a photograph etc.' in a span of twenty years of work.

"Shall I put on Bach?" she asked him.

"If you wish".

And he remembered that specific piece of music in the middle of the desert, the music of a wind instrument, a young man with eyes the colour of honey, blowing into the barrel, and another man accompanying him with the bayonet and a black helmet when…

"They've put the gramophone on again…"

"For God's sake!"

"Patience!"

"She sits for hours glued to the window, without even listening..."

"If she could at least hear it!"

"She's grown old and dull, a cantankerous expectant! Let it be far from us! Till the day she gives birth, the juice she'll be left with will be the juice she will lose".

"Not that he's any better!"

"I can see you're doing better..." Demetriades dared answer numbly to Joseph's hearty handshake.

"Indeed you are!" Father Stavros agreed. "I'm glad, Joseph dear!"

It was the first time in a while that he spoke to him with so much intimacy; and the priest's tone was fatherly.

Nicodemus served meze.

"On the house", he said. "My treat".

"Absolutely not!" Demetriades protested.

"I agree; why should it always be you?" Father Stavros concurred. "Let's go Dutch".

"Not another word", Nicodemus insisted. "I'll have no more of this; or else I'll have you pay for everything!"

They laughed and eagerly tasted the cured meats and sausages, all of them, except Joseph, who barely nibbled some cheese and two black olives.

"You're not eating! Go on, while it's still there", the priest urged him.

"I'm not hungry, thank you".

And he slowly swallowed the local red wine he had ordered.

"The prodigal son", he said with a smile.

"Why do you say that?" Father Stavros asked.

"This is who I am..."

They didn't ask him to clarify; it was obvious that he meant what he had said and it was bothering him. It was also true that, for months now, he had been avoiding them, hardly offering a "good morning" or a "good night", cold and stiff. He also happened to sit at the coffee shop, two or three times, without speaking a word more than necessary. They all thought he was ill or that his wife's illness had overpowered him. Others, including the priest, claimed that "his condition is to be equally blamed on his differences with the Agency and on inertia" – "What does he do now?" – "Rodi tells me he writes all day. She, on the other hand... Oh well, birds of a feather..." – "What's he writing about?" – "Lord knows!" – "A lot has befallen them! Once the storm begins..."

"Did you perhaps mention the 'prodigal son', dear Joseph, hoping Nicodemus would stoop to slaughter the fatted calf?" Father Stavros joked, eager to assign a soupcon of merriness to the gathering.

"Why not?" the shopkeeper replied. "There's only one Joseph Akritas in the village... He'd be worth it! But the calf we'll keep until the birth of young Akritas! Then we'll throw a big party and we'll have a ball!"

"Just be careful not to change your mind now that you've pledged", Kyros Demetriades smiled. "You'll lose a customer".

"Wait until the blessed time comes and you'll see the merit of Nicodemus!"

"Now that Nicodemus has mentioned it, when is the baby due?" Father Stavros asked the future father.

"I saw her the other day, Ms Maria, she looked just fine. Pregnancy becomes her; I think it'll be a big baby!"

"Yes!" Akritas muttered absent-mindedly.

"How far along is she?" Demetriades asked.

"She's eight months pregnant!"

The youngest son of Athanasis, the grocer, stepped into the coffee-shop. The boy had taken on the task of distributing mail. He approached Joseph and handed him a letter that made his face come alive. He apologized and opened it. It was written in German or French; rather... no, it was in English. Each of the men who had seen it would later offer a different opinion of its origin and language. The only certain thing was that it strongly moved the recipient who insisted on buying a round of drinks "for the good news" he unfortunately could not share for the time being.

In the afternoon, in the square opposite the 'Lovely Spilia', the touring circus came alive: three miracle workers, the 'Magicians', a giant who could bend and chew through iron, the 'Sirius', a pack of dogs of dubious races that danced and performed rhythmic gymnastics, a clown who played the guitar that sounded as a flute or the flute that sounded like pharyngeal serenades.

But the greatest impression of all was made by a middle-aged woman of around fifty, the exotic Maya Myrrha who had been in labour since the time she was twenty five. The baby simply wouldn't come out. Even more astonishing was the information the compère gave through the bullhorn that the parturient woman was able to converse with her twenty-five year old embryo! After a few indecipherable invocations that froze the blood of the villagers, and self-concentration for a few minutes, the woman asked her unseen 'child' if he wanted to talk to the village, "these kind people". He replied in a lad's voice, somewhat cavernous and distorted: "I would gladly answer any question".

"Just half a pound per question" warned the clown-compère.

Nicodemus spared the price: "Ask him why he sits in there and won't come out" he said, laughing.

The woman, sitting on a high black podium, placed her hands on her belly and repeated the question, then added: "Answer the gentleman, child".

The voice was heard loud and clear; they all heard it:

"Repent and I shall be born!"

Women in the audience made the sign of the cross; old woman Cleonice fainted.

"I had decided not to bother you with my own stuff. But today I can't help myself. I've learned something… something very pleasant! We've forgotten how to discuss the pleasant things… For various reasons which I will share with you at some point, a few months ago I began an experiment: to record the significant events I have witnessed as a photojournalist. Not the same exact events; their aftermath which is usually omitted. And what I started as an experiment gradually won me over! I am convinced that for every important news item there's an anti-news item; or scores of them. They're not always impressive, neither do they lend themselves to explanation, nor are they revealed unless you look for them, unless you scrutinize the cardinal information and reach its core. Not to mention that most of these news items ruin clear-cut lines for us and create a discordant polyphony within us, within all of us who are the down-to-earth majority, prejudiced in favour of the obvious, the exclusive and impressive; we feed on that, both literally and metaphorically. Anyway, to cut a long story short, all of a sudden I have discovered literature: anti-journalism. Even odder is the fact that Serghides himself gave me the first impulse. Much later, when I altered his initial suggestion in a manner that would satisfy and represent me, and mailed the first manuscripts to the Agency, I was certain they would reject them in line with their familiar decisions. So imagine my surprise today when I received this letter. They will publish my texts in a book. And they will pay every salary they had withheld from me. Can you believe it? What I've written is not just remote from classic journalism, it also exposes them! Neither do I predict the book will offer them any material profit. I was anticipating sarcasm with covert or bared irony, and suddenly this!"

"Why are you doing this? Why did you write this book? Who do you want to help?"

"Me, basically! But, as time goes by, my motives are improved. The pretext has led me to a series of causes. I have found a purpose, a new vision. And I'm fascinated by the hope that I'll be able to deliver it through a new prism".

"Which will be distorting again..."

"Why again?"

"Because it will be a lorgnette. They won't see the truth that had moved you in the first place".

"This will happen too, maybe later. Now the middleman is still indispensable. Just like you need the Archagielsks. And, unfortunately for them, others need me".

"...the face of the parturient woman hidden behind a dark arch-angel; her hands grasping two other angels, overaged, with femi-nine breasts, a man and a woman, and from the bleeding body..."

"...and the obstetrician, dressed in cyan, stands with an expres-sion..."

"...the hovering head with the steel four-rayed star fixed to the cranium, the neck, the ears, dominating at the centre of the wall-painting; the all-seeing eye; a miniature, a reflection of it, painted on each and every face of the wall-painting, either on the mantle, the eye, or the diadem, akin to a series of sparkles, shards ejected from the explosion..."

"This last phrase, albeit distinctive, should be omitted".

"You're right, I knew it. I thought it was nice, so I presumed it was redundant".

"Another glass of wine?"

"...a black framework, interrupted abruptly by the floor and roof; as if the wall and the roof are the boundaries of the world; or as if the roof and the floor of the world commence from this black framework..."

"This too should be rephrased; keep it as it is until 'the roof', more or less like this: "a black framework, terminating where the floor and the roof begin".

"What's the meaning?"

"What of?"

"Of the wall-painting".

"That remains to be seen".

"Don't you know already? Not even you?"

"Not yet".

....

"And the *'all-seeing eye'*. Erase that".

"I have already".

"Good! We'll keep it as it is until the *'centre of the wall-painting'*.

"What's the meaning of this dryness?"

"That remains to be seen".

"Don't you know already? Not even you?

....

"How many days yet?"

"As many as necessary".

"I'm scared".

....

"It becomes denser, then dissolves".

"Here! It's separated into its constituent parts".

"And it's perpetually recomposed of the parts into which it had dissolved".

She went back to writing, as if hypnotized:

  "...*like a piece of metal heavy heaviest a weightless snowflake and a flower sea star and then immediately a worm-like microbe embryo a moment of moving life a pulse and a rhythm hatched on its dome then the fluff the scale the nail and the tooth hunger and thirst and desire without a shape like a bush like a stain black expanding into a white infinite sun white into a black infinite moon and the haze and the ache and the twirling roar that becomes human the great subjugation and the beginning of the articulate howl my eumorphic amorphism my hopeless hope my hopeful utopia..."*

"Hosanna!"

Next morning, hunched over Avgi's wooden desk, Joseph worked on the foreword to his book.

"...try as I have, I'm unable to isolate the fact or facts that have led me to change, or the moment when change occurred. It's impossible, just like when you try to isolate that moment between your babyhood and childhood, when you made the leap from dispersed instinct to self-discovery. Therefore, I have had to restrict myself to conjectures in order to justify and explain the change I have experienced, conjectures that may partially explain it, but of course do not constitute a complete explanation. Perhaps it was brought on by the filterable virus of a thought, either mine or not, carried by something that had touched my spirit; an expression in the eyes of a child, amongst the countless I had seen through my lens; perhaps a sound from the intestines of a choleric man, now or years ago, that I knew would never reach the ears of those able to eradicate the disease, regardless of the tons of ink wasted by us, journalists and reporters; perhaps a hue of covert irony and analgesia in the

eyes of one of the very few who could untie the Gordian knot! Per-
haps the bars of gold out of poverty that had made him, but also
me, rich and famous, have offered me the certainty that those who
could align man's path have no need of updating or indications.
Nor do they intend to ever take relevant measures. They are aware
of what's essential: if they do it they will instantly stop being rul-
ers. Nevertheless, dear reader of my book, these are but conjectures.
The only thing that's certain is that from that very moment I lost
the most valuable thing I had: my naïve blissfulness!"

There was a knock at the door; it was time for her to come back
from the chapel. Today she was about half an hour late. But why
didn't she use her key? She does so every day. Today he'd give her
his manuscripts to read. He promised himself; he'd kindly ask for
her opinion, just like in the good old days.

He closed the dossier for a minute, then walked to the front
door.

It was Kyros Demetriades.

"I came by to say hello if you can spare a few minutes. I can come
back some other time if you're not free or available".

He told him he was welcome and showed him to the study.

"I'll sort out my notes while we speak".

"I'm interrupting, I'd better…"

"By all means! I'm done, I'll just put them in the trunk and I'm
all yours".

"Is Ms Akritas in?"

"Not yet. She won't be long".

"How is your work progressing?" Demetriades carried on, his gaze fixed on the manuscripts.

"I've actually finished, it's been a week now. I'll soon begin the final proof-reading".

"What's the title of your book?"

"THE OTHER SIDE".

"I imagine it'll be the first contribution of World News in the form of a book", said the Principal of the Spilia Elementary School, with a hidden pride afforded by the knowledge he was the first, in fact the only one in the village, in whom Akritas had confided about this particular project.

"In this specific sector, yes!"

"Would it be too much to ask you to let me read a small excerpt? Now that it's done..." he pleaded, guilty for being overbearing. "A short piece, a random excerpt".

Akritas looked into his eyes and allowed himself a faint, self-indulgent smile unlike his character.

"Is it so intriguing for you?"

"Need you ask?"

"Very well then!" And, opening the half-closed dossier, he randomly pulled out a page. He cast a quick look at it. "It's an excerpt from the African Journal", he said upon offering it.

Moved, Demetriades extended his arm. With his left hand he searched for his eyeglasses in his jacket. The small, somewhat dim characters of the typewriter wiggled and jumped about in front of him. He rubbed his eyes, then focused on the typewritten text:

...I might have been unlucky or lucky, I don't know which, and everything I have relayed here never occurred in my presence.What I have happened to experience, over and over again, was the mercenaries putting on the mask of the tough 'brass' each time they were informed I was in the area, lurking with cameras and microphones — which would prompt them to exaggerate in cruelty, what they called zeal for duty! Their aim was to provoke the omnivorous lens at any cost! Contemporary descendants of Herostratus! In the incident I'm about to recount, a Belgian corporal had been entrusted with delivering African Asian captives to Eritrea through the jungle — remains of what used to be human, emaciated from hunger and diarrhoea, dehydrated. As soon as I showed him my reporter's pass and authorization to freely move within war fronts, he systematically began provoking his prisoners with demonical inventiveness, became sadistic, tyrannical, "devoted to duty", until he achieved his goal: he had pushed them towards attempting to escape in spite of the risks and consequences. He'd even instructed his men to pretend they watched over them less rigidly, to relax their tight, spear-against-the neck guard.When one after the other the eight men crawled away under trees and weeds, he came to the inn and woke me up — it was two a.m. and cold — and he dragged me with him. First he made sure I was equipped with my camera and other tools. Four of the aspiring fugitives had been lanced on the spot, either as they clung to the barbed wire fencing or while hanging from it. There they stayed for days, hovering, prey to ravens and vultures. The fifth man had been decapitated outside the camp's perimeter, too weak to make a run for it. The remaining three were taken to the company's medical tent, abused, beaten, half-dead. Two months later, they were to be released. Newspapers and broadcast news had enough material for days. Some talked of the mercenaries' bestiality; regarding the macabre ending of the five; others, spoke of the heroism of the Belgian corporal who had risked his own life to eliminate the bloodthirsty terrorists. Others

opted for the philosophical standpoint, writing editorials on the ferocity and greatness of war! Herod's photographs were shown everywhere, different poses of the proponent of good order and protector of the rights of the white in Black Africa! But no one, including me, the self-righteous one, ever wrote eagerly and in length of the two doctors at the medical unit who, upon failing to secure blood for the badly wounded surviving victims of the 'heroic mercenary', plunged the syringes into their own arms. No one wrote that one of the two doctors died of excessive blood donation, shortly after the transfused patients had been released. It was only mentioned briefly and in passing…"

Demetriades removed his glasses, wiped them and gave back the page.

"We said one page", Akritas smiled after first casting a quick look at the paper and overwriting a few words with his pen. Then he added:

"I chose it at random, just like you'd asked. Both beginning and end are missing. It needs rephrasing and proofreading".

"There's nothing missing", Demetriades uttered, moved. He was silent for a while, then said: "I really can't understand your initial hesitations about having it published. These things are not meant to be kept in drawers…"

Akritas didn't answer; he got up and neatly placed the dossier with the manuscripts in the trunk.

"Are you publishing photographs too?"

"No, it would alter the character of the book, its intentions".

"Yes, maybe; you're right, I didn't think about that", Demetriades said. "In any case, it's…"

He cut himself short. The whole matter captivated him, but he shouldn't let his persistence make him annoying. He tried to change the subject, asked again about Maria, how she was these days.

"She's very well. Expecting…" Akritas smiled, adding: "What shall we drink?"

"Nothing, thank you. Isn't it enough that I've interrupted you?"

"On the contrary, I should've stopped a while ago. I've been working since five in the morning, I could definitely use a break; I've earned it".

"Never tiring!" the other man expressed his admiration.

"Not really… Just in a hurry".

He walked to the sideboard and took out a stool, decorated with star fish and shells, and two clay goblets. Then, a small plate with big raisins. He poured wine into the goblets.

"I will not drink to the success of the "Other Side", it's a given!" Demetriades raised the glass he was offered.

"I'm not so sure, dear Kyros! Neither of its potential success, nor my own motives, especially the latter!"

"Why do you say that?"

"Because with you I want to be honest. Believe me, there are times when I fear that I'm throwing myself into a pointless endeavour, an anachronistic and perhaps adventuristic one!… That I'm acting on an impulse; or that I'm growing old. Anyway, whatever the case might be, I'm determined to bring the book out. Therefore, everything else is only pharisaical!"

"You are wrong to doubt your decisions. These texts are tangible reality. They constitute an opus! And if they were pharisaic as you suggest, you should know they wouldn't bring out the results they have", Demetriades happily found himself back to the core of the matter that intrigued him so much.

"Which results are these?"

"You have transformed a provincial teacher into a rebel! And that's no little thing".

"You?"

"I've emulated you down to this very detail! You see... What you had confided in me kept me alert for days. It made me reconsider my whole life".

"And the conclusions?"

"Regardless of how much I have harmed my own self, I'm more responsible for the manner and the extent to which I have, for years now, been harming the children under my care. I have capitulated to a failed system of ideas and values which lacks the ingredients that could turn education into Pedagogy; we produce people willing, and perhaps able, to win over the world, even at the cost of losing their humanity..."

He went silent for a while, enough for him to sip some wine; then, he carried on:

"I'm afraid that if you were to vaccinate me some more with your anti-news, which mind you, I aspire to, I'll no longer be willing to go back to teaching. I'll give up my position and suffer the consequences".

"And what will you do if this were to occur?"

"I'll retire early, or attempt to found a school of my own, where I will be teaching what I consider to be fair and appropriate for my pupils".

"They'll shut you down on the second day!" Akritas smiled. "An endeavour like this is even more likely than mine to fail".

"Do you think so?"

"Yes! I do believe that gradually more and more people will be able to tolerate having the things I write published in newspapers and broadcast on TV!" and he glanced at the trunk. "But, to the best of my knowledge, no one in the foreseeable future would tolerate their children being vaccinated with ideas of this sort".

"But, precisely because…"

"Neither the family, nor the State, not even religion itself are ready to accept the consequences of our dehumanization, our efforts to sever our sharp edges. They're more afraid of good, what the few call good — freedom, love, logic — than evil. They can control evil, or so they think. What's good controls them".

"You are a doomsayer".

"I'm a realist".

"So, do you believe I stand to fail?"

"Yes! But I also know that if you have set out to do something like that, you won't give up, no matter what I say… You didn't come here for advice, you came to listen to my objections, which I'm sure you anticipated, to hone your defence system…"

"Perhaps! Perhaps you're right. Let's not forget I've always been cowardly and indecisive".

"Because you couldn't clarify what you really wanted. Now that you know what you want, you'll shed your objections…"

"I wish it be so! If I can achieve that, which I doubt, I'll be the first graduate of my school".

"Here's to it!"

The bell rang.

"Excuse me, it should be Maria".

"By all means!" Kyros Demetriades replied and walked to the window.

He heard the door open and the voice of Piotr Archangielsk. Then the door closed and Joseph Akritas came back to the room. His face ashen, voice shivering:

"The pain is excruciating!"

"I've added two to your drink, just two; they're harmless, your doctors' instructions. They're optimistic, more than at any other time. For three hours they were examining you with every means available to them. And the menisci, some bright or radioactive menisci, I'm not exactly sure of their nature, that recently appeared in your X-rays, have either absorbed or dissolved the largest part of the tumours. Isn't this wonderful? I for one, Maria, never doubted you would beat this. And today I am vindicated! Yes, I did contact the nurse on duty. I also spoke with Dr Herodotou. In a bit, they said. They're preparing your room. It's east-facing, with plenty of light and a view of the mountain. Yes, they're both downstairs, in the Waiting Room. They notified me, him; he came running from the chapel. I'll let them know, don't worry. Now I need you to relax. Shall I ask the nurses for another painkiller? Alright... In a bit. You're sweating. Here, let me wipe it. One more pillow? There you go! What was I saying? Oh, yes... Tomorrow I deliver the book. They're satisfied, and so am I. I can't wait for you to read it, tell me what you think. I intended to give it to you but events got the best of me. I'm doing this for you, Maria, not for me, regardless of what I'd said or done. Back then, I'm afraid I wasn't... I guess I wasn't

myself, what's the point in hiding it from you? Do you want to
hear the absolute truth? The only thing I won't put up with is
losing you; and the only thing I will accept as justice for the life I
have lived so far, is for you to stay with me. They're identical, it's
tautology, I know, but it's the truth! You are the most beautiful,
grandest thing that has ever happened in this long, insignificant
life of mine! I'm neither exaggerating nor ruminating others'
words. It's just how it is. And... your child. I love it, expect it,
in spite of what I said the other day. I did and said so many things
I didn't mean, or things I meant at the time but no longer do.
They were clouds that went away. From the moment I decided
to emulate you in secrecy, lest you suspected something, I was
able to stand back on my feet. My own two feet, as if my feet
were my soul and the entire world! I found myself and you. And
a path to tread, a destination! I had hidden this from you when
I informed you of my decision to start writing this work, this
opus according to the eloquent Demetriades – the reason why
I was doing it, the main cause! It was to become worthy of you,
to win you back, to declare my emotions with actions, to win
back your trust, the trust of the mother of my child. You see,
now I dare say what I was afraid of. Because that's the truth.
Your child is also my child. And this I'm asking you to believe.
Do you believe me? Don't answer now. Later. Or never, if you
wish. I'm not expecting assurances from you. As long as you are
aware of it. And I'm going to tell you something else, the main
piece of anti-news I've obtained, a genuine exclusive. Joseph
and Maria are expecting. Zero plus zero equals everything. Their
son! Look, the nurse is here. She'll take you now. I'll be waiting
for you here. Yes, I'll go down and talk to them. Have a... safe
delivery".

The lobby before the Operating Room; "To Obstetrics Room";

immersed in milky white light; the telephone's crimson eye emitting messages; the nurse presses the button and answers; mute words.

Joseph, sat on a white leather chair next to the entrance to the hallway; apathetic.

On two white leather chairs near him, Piotr and Hanna: "Hanna and the Hun!" – who was it that first called them that? Wholesome, blending into the white; and serene, as if peacefully departed.

"How much more?" someone asks the nurse, perhaps them or him, probably him. Or a third party!

She has this stain, like a black spot on her white robe. A birthmark or cancer… She seems to be answering the question; vaguely so. He can't hear.

Someone else spoke. Either a man or a woman.

"Can I smoke?"

Again, no sound, though a retort followed, forbidding. The smoker, cross, walks out onto the veranda.

Piotr approaches Joseph.

"Can I have a word with you?"

The voice infiltrated him like a surge. He replied something he couldn't hear.

"It will soon be time for us to say goodbye. Today we completed the task assigned to us. We're returning the keys to the chapel and the *anoi* tonight. We won't see each another again. Perhaps! Or after…"

Years or centuries?

Hanna closes in.

"Today is the new beginning of your life. And ours, all of us who are suffering".

"Today we enter the Age of the Aquarius" he adds. "Today it shall rain blood!"

"It has been for years now..."

"Ever since..."

"She, the Bloodbearer..."

They reach out their hands to him, he takes them unwillingly into his. Into his two hands. Or into their four, or eight hands. Or even... A tremor... He can't feel any hand being thrust under his cold, frozen fingers. As if he'd been reaching out to a nightmare that had already pervaded his gut, stirring and detaching; and washing it off with...

"Thank you", he offered.

He more felt than heard his voice, like a cold gust of wind rolling down his aching throat.

Inside! Inside! Yes, inside, now, now inside voices were heard, inside, inside where? – what kind of orders, cries and rearrangement of organs and hopes? Inside... Across the entire en....

...ORMOUS AMPLIFIER, AN ENORMOUS AMPLIFIER HER life, encapsulated into this sharp,sharpest and torturous closure of pleasure or the pleasurable closure of torture; she was no longer in a position to name and justify; doused within the blinding light that was born and emitted of her body, the transfiguration and transformation had already begun. Swirls of light, akin to flowers with in finite petals had broken her brain apart, akin to opium daisies, her throat and sternum, they had trans muted her into pulp: white, golden and azure first, then flowing matter, trans lucent of cyan white yellow with infinite meta-bol-isms of colours; that though shapeless themselves contained all shapes, all forms, contrast-ed for infinity.

And her mother, m-other, came, hair dishevelled, and she leant over and sank her hands, soiled with wastewater and jasmine and tahini and plucked feathers from a rooster, into the pulp of the sternum, inside, inside her, made the sign of the cross and left, holding her dead child in her arms, a slaughtered lamb: "Blessed art thou!"

And her father, f-ather, came, dressed in black and a khaki jacket. He caressed the edges of her hair, air, brought his arm to his kepi, reverently removed it, leant over to kiss her hand; in a Calvariae Locus inside her she saw him pierced all over, empty, down to his soles; an un-processed hu-man tube; he left, sobbing, holding tufts of her hair like a talisman and plunder, a fetish: "Blessed art thou!"

And Joseph came and lay down next to her, xt to her, and held within his hands her hand, and a thousand hands. And suddenly his fingers became cold and harsh, either metals or scales, and his entire skin, akin to a fish a reptile or an insect, acquiring the hues of copper. And underneath that heavy arm-ament he was shout-ing and ple-ading; but the voice was lost in its rev-er-berations, his in deci-, in-decisive-ness, a blend of several sounds anni-hi-lating one an-other. "Blessed art thou!"

And Michael came, with overaged angels, els, two, on his right and left, tacit-urn, nude, their silver white beards reaching down to their feet and one of them was male, with a gigantic pelvis -vis reaching down, and the other one was female, with full, smooth breasts akin to ala-baster; and all of a sudden the archangels em-b-raced him, first the male; and immediately he was absorbed; then the female; and she was absorbed with a roar reminiscent of the murmur of surging waters coming together. And from arms and legs and all joints, hers or his, the sound of a flute or guitar emerged and enfolded her, thickening the terrible passions of the world and her soo-thed like the pro-mise of heaven yearning to appease and trans figure them; a treasure for You... And he came closer and told her: "Beloved!" And his voice was the voice of a thousand guitars chanting together within the swell of the celest-ial void that was repl- with promi and sleepless, invisible, seven-coloured rays carrying six rays each. He lay near her -ar her. Next to. And a drill of alabaster lily penetrated vagina, smooth, lavish green, cutting through the grass, chlo- rophyll. And she turned and kissed the eyes. And said: "Beloved!" And the sublime, the, dr- ill, un and un and unfolded within the vagina, became a funnel and akin to an oviduct great or a tuba or, and with a contraction of his chest and a kiss on the li, he poured inside her the seed of the gigantic testicles; she was im-mersed; short of breath, her te-ars in sockets. With a howling of torture, rupture and pleasure she opened the warm crimson gates of the uterus to absorb it instantly, ravenously, the way dried earth drinks the first rain... "Blessed art thou!"

Then at once the two bright white angels slipped out of his body, were separated and became young and fair like juveniles and like Him, knelt before him and called him "Ancient!" They kissed the yellow sandals, the azure daisy on his mantle. And then, once and for all, the light, like a full stop, at the heart of the pyrite was en-livened, the fervent spike of a cosmic ray and began digging into her heavy most hea-vy volume. A sharp four-rayed shard that rose towards every possible direction then became eight-rayed, sixteen-rayed and and and was mu-lti-plied and raised to the nth power, always preserving within, always within its core the childlike form with the azure eyes she had once seen on a wall painting and there were so many and so blinding those infinite angelic heads that emerged, a beam within a beam, incessantly, and spread out freely, as if an explosion had splintered her very core, a libation at the centre of the cranium within the multi-scented ov-oid pulp that was her entrails; and she felt vast love en-gulfing her her her, wisdom and awareness indescribable, as if that polymorphous pulp was the absolute the great eye for any time, any space and any toil, as if it absorbed and stored the laws of the abyss and as if that first shard of light was the entire world ex-ploded and satu-rating her becoming an indi-visible whole with her body and spirit; as if every fibre of hers were a vagina and every ray an angel's tube that set off within her springs of ce-lestial seed. And she felt innumerable lips quenching their thirst from her love, in infinite forms of hers carved on flesh, her flesh, on stone, her stone, on metal, her metal, on wood, her wood, and sharing with her the sacrament of communion, as she shared with them her sanctum sanctorum.

And she knew now that as soon as she'd open her mouth and expire, an exhalation of wisdom and love, a stupor of freedom would begin and last for as long as the world would last for her. And her life thereafter. Or for two thousand years! The twenty centuries of the Aquarium! And she wouldn't open her mouth. She would hold the scream inside of her, grinding it. But she could no longer hold out...

...the obstetrician leant over her, exuding care; so did the nurse, dressed in white; they wiped the sweat off her eyebrows and cheeks.

"Now, Maria, now! It will be a big, great boy! Or a girl. Or..." He smiled at her awkwardly. The members of the Medical Council drew closer.

They clearly heard her say:

"I'm delivering my salvation!"

HER EXHALATION, EITHER A SCREAM OR A CARESS, IN-
specting his entrails like blinding light, electrifying nebula, pain,
sweet to the eyes he was struggling to keep wide open, to his
disjointed joints, inside his distended heart. To the very core. The
core! Vertigo, an explosion, hedonic convulsions of the marrow,
of tumors and vessels. And so for the first time he became one
with his body and spirit. An identification painful and hedonic
within a crimson peak that was humid and smooth, and received
all of him, drained him, a huge egg of prehistoric beast or arch-
angel, golden and bright white, and amidst shudders, shivers and
convulsions, like a gigantic phallus, the sperm poured out of the
slit of an enlarged head, like a glans, out of eyes, lips, nostrils,
onto her body, onto his body, like masturbation, like copulation,
like a panhedonic stream of consciousness inwards and everywhere; towards the void filled by the new self-awareness.

"I'm afraid it's urgent!" the nurse said on the phone behind the
screen. "Please, doctor, you should come immediately! I think
he's suffered an epileptic episode... When the scream was heard
from inside the room! He jumped right up, drenched in sweat,
his entire body shivering. I even think there's something... on
him... either sperm or urine. You must see him. The two strangers are holding him on either side. Come, please! Here! He's...
Mr Akritas, don't... You're not allowed, sir".

He went on, dragging the Archangielsks with him towards the
Delivery Room. The glowing sign: " ". But he didn't stop. The
white door was closed. He pushed it lightly. It opened wide. On

his right and left, akin to wings, Him and Her. On their right and left, through them, between them, the doctors and the nurses and the assistants were taking their leave. White silhouettes, masks of gauze. One after the other. Whispers in the fog:

......

".........................."

......

"..."

".............................."

".................................."

".................................."

On the operating table, covered with a white sheet, a black tuff of hair escaping from the mound and a pool of blood outlining the rigid body.

There was no movement or progress.

None!

He stood over her.

"You can do this!" he told her.

He reached out his hand, uncovered her. In front of him...

" "

It was him! Naked! Rigid! Exposed before his very eyes.

"If you have love".

THE DIRECTOR OF THE POLYCLINIC SAW HIM WITH AN hour's delay. He was chewing on his half-extinguished cigar, spitting bits out into the crystal polyhedron ashtray in front of him. In the surrounding armchairs, in rigid, orthopaedic postures, the pathologist, the obstetrician, the biochemist, the anaesthesiologist, the elderly family physician of the Akritases.

"Have a seat", he said. Long pause. Protracted coughing. "I'm afraid I'll be a doom…"

The anaesthesiologist, though it didn't become him at all, dryly coughed too; he was young, square, modern, with an Ashton Martin and a pilot's license. But he too revealed great awkwardness and distress; him, and not the seventy year old family physician.

"…a doomsayer once more", Dr Herodotou completed his sentence.

They all spoke in an uncoordinated and disorderly manner.

"Unfortunately".

"In spite of everyone's best efforts…"

"Our superhuman efforts…"

"And even though we had applied all available means…"

"In any case, there was no hope of survival for your wife", the pathologist interrupted Dr Herodotou.

"In spite of indications to the contrary", the obstetrician added.

The anaesthesiologist sat up and coughed again. Dr Herodotou puckered his lips, chewed on the cigar some more and spoke again:

"Something unprecedented happened, and indeed unexplainable! My esteemed colleagues here may well confirm my words. Even though a normal pregnancy was clinically verified by all and at every stage that developed smoothly, despite the particularities of the case, it was nevertheless proven eventually that... Or rather not. It was of course a form of pregnancy, gestation without...I find it difficult to put into words. And whilst during labour everything progressed completely normally, neither during nor after the ensuing loss of fluids... There was simply no... there was no... Gestation or... It was a kind of pseudo-pregnancy, followed by pseudo-labour. Because, in the course of labour, if such a term could be applied to this case, the after-effects of a normal delivery had occurred: full dilation, relaxation, bleeding... In the case at hand the bleeding was unstoppable, persistent and painful. Even the fall of the umbilical cord, a cord that was not attached to an infant mind you, and which is normally cut; by normally I mean... So you do understand our confusion. With all this..."

"It's as if the unseen has been born... with the properties and dimensions of the ordinary: volume, weight, resistance".

"My dear colleague, I beg to differ! Anything but ordinary: it was unnaturally big, hence the bleeding! Afterwards... when she was weighed, she was found to be lighter by 110 pounds!"

"You do understand the problem".

"Its dimensions".

"So unexplainable it was that if we were to announce it, given the lack of a precedent or any scientific interpretation, we would appear..."

"Let's be blunt, dear colleagues. We would appear ridiculous!"

"Mercifully we were all there!" Dr Herodotou resumed. "And all present are acclaimed scientists, with extended experience in our respective field of expertise. Even more important is the fact that we were fully cognizant of your wife's particular case. Naturally, there must be some scientific explanation, and we intend to seek it. In the meantime I would kindly ask you not to disclose any information pertaining to what has transpired here. You do realize the delicacy of the situation and the adversities we are about to face. However, this will not be indefinite, only until a general scientific inquiry is made and until all of us here are able to jointly provide a comprehensive report on the issue at hand".

"No objection. We're all in agreement", the anaesthesiologist added.

Joseph lifted his gaze and looked at them, one by one; they lowered theirs. Only Dr Herodotou returned his gaze behind the cigar.

"She delivered what she'd received", Joseph Akritas murmured as if hypnotized.

Someone knocked; then the assistant medical examiner rushed inside the room. He delivered an envelope, and secretly whispered something into the ear of his superior before leaving as quickly as he had come. The medical examiner handed the closed envelope to Dr Herodotou, who opened it with obvious uneasiness. A wrinkle carved deep into his forehead as he read the report and examined the accompanying X-rays. Then he gave the envelope to the biochemist.

"Not even one! Not a single trace! She's fully, completely healed! And the menisci have been reinforced, here!" and leaning over the X-Rays pointed to what he meant.

"In fact, they are in full bloom!"

"With cells and colours arranged in a ray-like form resembling... fans!"

"That meniscus there is new! There, like a rising sun behind the uterus".

"It seems to me that with her death, Ms Akritas..." the Director of the "Hygeia" Polyclinic began saying once the reports and X-rays had been passed from one doctor to another until they all saw them – and looked for Joseph among them; but he wasn't there. He had slipped out of the room.

As soon as the news spread, and in small villages bad news like this spreads like wildfire, Father Stavros had two choir boys summon the two of them, the Principal of the Elementary School and Nicodemus. He was waiting for them at the church guest-house, anxious. They found him steaming with rage. Without any preludes he declared he had decided and knew what to do and how to do it.

"When did... you find out, Father?"

"When did I find out what, Kyros?"

"That she... Is she really... Is she..." Demetriades stuttered.

"A short while ago; my youngest daughter called me, she's at the "Hygeia", about to give birth. She died in labour, bled to death. Her baby is dead too; decomposed".

"I can't imagine how Mr Akritas should feel", Nicodemus muttered.

"Obliterated, how do you expect him to feel?"

"Ever since those two came to our village there hasn't been one sunny day!"

"It's over now, Nicodemus. I'll kick those Jews out of here once and for all, otherwise I stand to do much worse, now in my old age!"

"Keep your calm, Father. You're a man of the cloth!"

"And I'm holding a scourge!" the other man replied and walked on. "Come".

Half willing and half unwilling, they followed him, as one of them swallowed his wrath, the other his objections. They first knocked at the *anoi*; there was no answer. They tried again, at the back door.

"Father Stavros, stop! Master Nicodemus! We'll rouse everyone in Spilia".

"They're probably at the chapel".

They rushed down the stairs and got into Father Stavros' jeep, parked in the alley across the street. The priest, agile, sat behind the wheel. Next to him sat Nicodemus, Demetriades in the back seat, amidst tools and buckets. With a groan the engine sprang to life, grinding dust. It bounced up and down the dirt road, as if flying.

As the sun gleamed its last rays, the chapel glowed peacefully, like a vision amidst the hills. Pristine yard, whitewashed walls, a new door, as yet unpainted, flower beds with dahlias and wild roses next to the fence.

The priest jumped out of the jeep and banged repeatedly against the door with his fists.

"They're not in", Demetriades said with relief.

"They've locked themselves inside! Open the door!" the priest commanded. There was no answer. "I'll break it open".

"Here, I'll help", said the butcher.

They grabbed the iron bar and pick from the jeep.

It took three blows for the door to open, to be torn apart. They got in through the hole. Something fluttered in the dim light.

"They're not here, Father".

...

"Go look inside the bema".

...

"In the vestibule, at the front".

...

"Behind the pews".

...

"Down at the holy water spring".

...

"There's just a pigeon, a sparrow and... and a..."

"Speak, butcher!"

"A goldfinch. They sat on my shoulder".

"Grab them!"

"I have".

"Here's a cord, tie them up".

"I've tied them up".

"They keep a spotlight projector somewhere in here".

"Here it is".

"Turn it on. You show him, Kyros".

Light shone over the sacred world of the wall-painting that only the previous day had been restored in its entirety, from top to bottom; from the point where the raw beams touched the roof down to the beginning of the worn out slabs on the floor. And in the crowded centre: overaged angels, female ones, and men in cloth, their beards reaching down to their navels, surrounding the Mother. At the back, Joseph, headless, and next to him a priest holding a pickaxe, a clerk with an empty sheet of paper, and a peasant without eyes, ears and tongue; with a cavernous mouth and hairy skin. Further back, a figure, head sunk into the shoulder, and another man with a pierced sternum. A shepherd and whores and tax collectors and men possessed. Around them, over them, under them, everywhere, akin to an explosion of rays, big and small heads of an adolescent man, his ornament a four-rayed steel star.

"The Nativity!" the teacher whispered. "The Nativity without the divine infant! Unless, unless it's... Unless the divine infant is this set of dispersed... Father Stavros, this is a masterpiece, it's ingenious!"

"This is blasphemy!" the priest lashed out on him. "This is not a divine birth, it's a birth that's satanic!"

"It's… I'm telling you, this is unique. It's a revelation, it will cause a great stir! Mark my words", Demetriades, ecstatic, carried on his soliloquy.

"It's a trap, the work of the devil! They're Jews, aren't they? They applied sorcery to draw it, working in secrecy over these past nine months. Her death is their doing! Just like the disappearance of Avgi and the death of the infant! But I will wreak havoc upon both of them and their blasphemy, their witchery!"

And clenching the iron bar, he shoved it into the centre of the representation as if into a warm belly.

"What are you doing! Have you lost your mind, Father? Stop!" Demetriades protested, strongly, fiercely.

And he ran towards him. But the priest pushed him away with his elbow and the iron bar. He threw him down; then he lunged again. Around his feet, two multi-coloured fragments came down scattered.

"For God's sake, it's a sin!" the Principal whispered.

Getting to his feet, he tried to stop them.

"Go away, Kyros", Nicodemus, ferocious, blocked the way with his body.

In vain he pleaded; in vain he threatened; for the sake of the wall-painting, for art, for the village which would be irreparably damaged, for him, for friendship and whatever it was that bound them to one another.

Nothing of what he said worked; his pleadings were mere bouts of hysteria and annoyance.

"Take him outside, butcher; he's busting my balls".

Within a short while, ten to twelve minutes, the entire painting, the entire plaster, was reduced to a pile of dyed shards underneath their feet.

All that was left was white void staring at them, a deadly wounded wall where the enigmatic figures lay for centuries, a white that was emptier than the black enwrapping it from floor to ceiling.

Once they rested under the shade of the tall alders and drank water from the spring, Father Stavros felt hungry; he stood up, clasped the three birds and ripped their heads off. He plucked them, picked up a fresh branch, sharpened it with his pocket knife, impaled them and sprinkled them with wine from his flask.

"Fire", he commanded Nicodemus.

"I can see you're fully prepared, Father" the other man said, lowering a match amidst the underbrush.

Once the two of them ate – Demetriades refusing to so much as touch anything – and drank all the wine from the flask, they got into the jeep.

"Now let's pursue our search in Kakopetria or Platania!" the priest said. "I'm livid. If I find them, by God, I'll kill them! I loved her as a daughter. Avgi too!"

Upon their return to the village, late at night, they heard the news; the Archangielsks, either because they had lit a fire to cook birds next to the Gate, or because they forgot the spotlight projector on, had caused the chapel to burn to the ground.

All that was left standing were four walls, bare and blackened, and a heat so strong that no one could go near.

.

FIRST DAY AFTER THE INTERNMENT. MORNING.

The nurse, dressed in white, knocked on the door for a second time. She persisted. He was there, she'd seen him going in.

Dr Herodotou's voice:

"Yes, come in, please".

Just as she'd expected; she found him just as he was the day before and during the entire night, carefully comparing the X-rays and the reports of the medical examiner, the chemist and the special cytologist.

"Excuse me, Dr Herodotou".

"Yes, what is it now?"

"I'm not sure whether it's something which…if it is of interest to you. I assumed I had to let you know".

"What's wrong? Quickly, please!" he cut in.

"I don't know how to explain it. All the rose bushes lining the entry to the Clinic…"

"Well?"

"They're all in bloom! This rare variety you brought from your travels; it never blossoms before May, at the earliest!"

"Is this why you've interrupted me?"

"Well, it's not May... and..."

"Yes! That's right! So? Is that all?"

"And their scent, it's different. It's not just me, the patients have noticed it, visitors too! Even passers-by, they just stop and stare. But what's even stranger..."

"Yes, go on!"

"...is their colour! It's the most vibrant, most unusual hue I've ever seen! And it seems to be diffused, and..."

"Well?"

"...it radiates, just like the menisci in the X-rays of Maria Akritas..."

The doctor's gaze was reinvigorated.

"Full report, please. Analysis, cell structure, arrangement of elements etc. And have the roses sent to the Lab".

"Here you are!" the nurse smiled. "We took the initiative to send them to the Lab as urgent... given your particular interest in the case".

Without replying, he took the X-rays and reports the nurse had placed before him and began juxtaposing them fervently. Half an hour of thorough study.

Then he picked up the phone anxiously and dialled.

"The doctor, please. Thank you. Yes, it's me, Dr Herodotou, it's urgent. I'll wait. Hello Thrasyvoulos, yes! Now here's the icing on the cake!"

And he went on to relate the new developments in detail:

"The same crystalloid form of cells, the same spherical arrangement in groups, congruent radiation etc. And the same distinct scent of lavender. No! Not lavender, myrrh! Certainly... You can see them right now, come over. Bring the others too. No, there's no need to repeat the test, the similarity is more than evident, it's identical! Yes, you're right! That's not a bad idea, as long as they can be convinced. The husband and close friends, precisely, her inner circle. Also, the two conservators. Wait a minute; why not us too? The two of us and the other three attending physicians. Yes, everyone present. After all, we all felt it. Either by touch or by reflection it was transmitted. I for one, ever since that moment, have the feeling I'm inhabited by someone else. Exactly. I'll call them to come here the soonest possible for an autopsy. Bye for now!"

And he hung up. Only then did he realize the nurse was still in his office.

"You too!" he told her.

"Yes?"

"Nothing! Later. And I depend on your discretion!"

SECOND DAY. MORNING.

He awoke with a strong urge. Today he wouldn't give in. This day would not be the same as yesterday or the day before, another repetition of all the days he had spent in Spilia and before that, in his home village and in Morphou, at the Teachers College; of the days he hadn't really lived, but merely let sway him into their own sluggish spin, a swirl so concentric and eurythmic, that it had become pointless – and so now he approached old age from the dim route of negotiating denials.

He had been a teacher from as far back as he could remember. He has no memory of a day when he was something else; always calm, polite, compromising. There had never been a day when he was genuine and true to his essential self, when he had said what he preferred to say, what he had on his mind, when he was less calm, less polite, less condescending and more consistent with the man he really was: less sugar and more salt. He cannot remember ever laughing or crying to a point of being cleansed. His laughter and weeping were one and the same: a hypotonic, subdued stutter. And the causes that brought them to the surface were trifling and quotidian; not borne of the sluggish conscience lying deep within him.

But today! When he awoke today, his decision had already been confirmed, finalized, harsh and processed like a diamond. He will not yield! He will exit his orbit, live, laugh or cry beyond average. When did he change so? How did the wall he had been building for decades, sacrifice after sacrifice, collapse within just a few hours without so much as causing him to jolt, flutter? It was as if the casing of his consciousness had caved in inside him and he became possessed by a new spirit that was insubordinate and sharp, with well-aimed rays akin to steel intended to dissolve and discard everything he had accumulated in the ascetic sacristy of his soul.

And now he was, God, so... He was alive! Alive! He was alive though he hadn't lived yesterday, nor did he care about whether he would be alive tomorrow or... But now...

He got dressed and left the house that was stifling him. He picked a carnation and fixed it to his lapel – for the first time in the thirty years he had been growing them precisely for this purpose. He went to the 'Lovely Spilia', ordered coffee; he finished it without talking to anyone, merely nodding silent hellos two or three times, just as he had wanted to do for years now but talked instead, when all he yearned for was to be quiet and relish the sounds. He paid for the coffee and returned to the street on foot, passing by the Coed Elementary School without so much as pausing or wavering, picked up a peach tree branch from the berm and carried on in good spirits. When the bell tolled for the Morning Prayer of the Cyclamens, he had already covered three kilometres on the road to Kakopetria.

"I came to give a statement", he told his friend the sergeant who'd seen him invading the Police Station with a huge flower fastened to his lapel.

"Now what? Someone burnt down the school?"

"Not yet".

The sergeant ordered two coffees – "Wake up, Loizos!" he told his sleepy assistant.

"Well?"

"Regarding the chapel".

The sergeant sat up. It was an open case, threatening to cost him the promotion and transfer to the city which until the day before yesterday was almost guaranteed. If he didn't solve the case and fast, the only guaranteed transfer would be exile to God knows where...

He took the envelope the Principal offered him.

"The Chapel of the Three Young Men?"

"Is there another one?" Demetriades answered the question. "I have recorded the facts in every detail".

"And how do you know what happened there, Kyros?"

"I was an eye witness; more or less. And in a sense I was also an accomplice".

"You what?"

"And Nicodemus. Father Stavros too".

"Unbelievable!" exclaimed the sergeant after reading the report. "Have they lost their minds? And you couldn't bring them to their senses?"

"You know how Father Stavros is. Once roused, he's bound and determined!"

"Anything else?"

"Nothing", Kyros murmured absent-mindedly.

The sergeant stood up, removed his glasses and cast a cautious look at his friend:

"You do realize this is serious stuff…" he said. "They're infuriated at Headquarters and the Museum. I'll come to the village at noon or early afternoon to take statements. Will you be there? I'll need you. Do the others know you were going to come here to report them?", and he glanced at the confession.

"They didn't".

"Then please, keep it that way for the time being".

"Yes".

"Shall I ask Loizos to drive you back?"

"No, I'd rather walk".

"Suit yourself. By the way, are schools closed today?"

"I took a day off".

He walked back to the village by around eleven o'clock. Two kids, schoolbags underarm, were playing marbles in the middle of the street. As soon as they caught sight of him, they stopped and stood aside, as if he were… They said hello sir, though they couldn't believe their own eyes. Either something was seriously wrong or the Principal had lost… his marbles.

He called out to them amicably, greeting them by name which he oddly remembered this time, paused, bent down, picked up a marble that had rolled between his feet, black with a white dot, aimed at the other boy's marble; bull's eye!

He laughed.

"And to think I haven't played marbles in some thirty years", he said.

The boy approached him and gave him back the marble; he affectionately stroked the child's hair, aimed again. The glass ball carved a streak of light along its orbit until it crashed against the second marble that lay at a distance of five yards, splitting it in two with a sharp tingle.

"He's really good at this!" the boys said as he set off.

He didn't enter the school, nor his house. Nor did he turn to secretly take pride in his garden, like he used to do, as he passed outside. He went straight to the house of Ioulia Michaelidou. He knocked at the door, heard indistinct noises, words coming towards him shapeless, either hers or broadcast on the radio; then, footsteps.

"Who is it?"

"It's me".

She opened the door, surprise spread across her face.

"You left without notice... For a minute I was worried".

"May I?" he asked.

"Yes, of course. Do come in".

They sat in the living room. It was replete with flowers, dahlias and branches. All around the room, roses and lilies and sea stars, either drawn or embroidered on the sofa cover, the cushions, the paintings she had made herself. At the corner, her monogram in purple thread: I.M.

"What's wrong?" she asked him.

"Something urgent came up, near here. It's done now. Am I keeping you from lunch?"

"No, I'm almost finished. Would you care to join me?"

"Gladly!"

His response added to her surprise and awkwardness. She ran to the kitchen to get a second serving, and to "freshen up", she said.

He followed her, after giving her two or three minutes to get ready. He was hungry. Walking had given him an appetite. She served pilaf – rice with mushrooms – and beef filet. He opted for salad and cheese, and a piece of lean filet.

"You're very frugal!" Ioulia Michaelidou remarked. She had the impression he was more of a glutton.

"I'm going to start dieting!" he replied. "In two months I'll drop twenty pounds".

"That many!" she marvelled. "You're really determined".

"Not really, but I will be. The more pounds I drop, the more determined I will become".

In spite of her objections, he helped her do the dishes.

Then, "in exchange for his humiliation and trouble", as he good-humouredly put it, he wouldn't say no to coffee; not too sweet, just a teaspoon of sugar; rather – no sugar!

"Are you certain?"

"Absolutely!"

They moved to the parlour and had coffee in silence. She cast secret glances at him, at a loss as how to explain his behaviour. Yes, now she was positive; he was a different man, almost unknown to her. But so agreeable, so desirable! This is how she had envisioned the same Kyros she had known until yesterday without ever hoping her secret expectations to bear fruit…

"You have changed" she dared say.

"For the worse?" he laughed.

"Not at all! For the better, of course…"

"Why 'of course'"?

"I don't know. Maybe…"

"Even though I assigned responsibility for the entire school to you, without due notice?" he cut in, relieving her of her embarrassment.

"Maybe that's why!" she smiled. "How did you do that?"

"I don't know. I went to bed as two different persons and woke up as one".

"I don't understand".

"Neither do I, at least not fully. Last night I was still the person I'd always been. I went to sleep with everything I had appropriated, all the things I had wrapped myself in. Then, all of a sudden, don't ask me how or why or exactly when, I lost my swaddling clothes, and all that was left behind was me, a bare Me…"

"That's marvellous!" said the young woman.

"I've really changed, haven't I? Beyond recognition!"

"Yes, I mean, I…"

"I've always been like this, deep down. I just wouldn't allow myself to show it".

"How do you feel? I mean…"

"Wonderful! Sounds a bit naïve, doesn't it? Let me rephrase; I feel free, freer, disengaged. I term things by their proper name and act accordingly".

"That's why…"

"Precisely. That's why I invaded your house and imposed myself upon you. That's why I can speak to you so openly".

"What if… and this is a hypothetical question, what if the others don't approve?"

"I will not insist. This new state of immoderation I'm indulging in (and I do hope I will keep on indulging in, I do hope it's not just a temporary, seasonal eclipse of my propriety) is not at odds with discretion. If I'm correct in interpreting what is happening to me and how things will evolve from now on, I will not try to either directly or indirectly make anyone do anything; nor do I intend to be free at the expense of others".

"What do you mean?"

"If my own freedom either hurts or belittles you, feel free to say it. I will insist no further. The same applies to anyone else. You see, in this sense, it's not really immoderation".

"No it's not, in this sense", and she faltered.

"What is it? What's bothering you?" he encouraged her.

"Alright. I wanted to ask… why after what has happened to you, did you choose to come to me?"

"Because this is what I've always wanted to do; to come here and confide in you that I can no longer live by myself, nor can I imagine myself being anywhere else but here. That I want to call you by your first name and hold your hand, hold you in my arms if you want it too, I want to lie next to you and live with you for as long as we shall both want to; forever or for a while. Now it's up to you to tell me, to ask me to go away and never dare talk to you again, never again take advantage of the friendship you have offered me".

"Or?" she asked.

"Or you can give me your hand and I will take in the whole of you".

There was a moment of silence; then Ioulia reached out her hand and placed it in Kyros' palm. Their touch invigorated their skin and eyes, it made the two of them white and humble, for themselves and for the entire...

THIRD DAY, AFTERNOON; AVGI RETURNED.

Joseph Akritas went through the laconic letter once more before signing it:

Dear Mr Serghides,

I would like to inform you that I have irrevocably decided to re-sign from my post at the World Press and News Agency. The pertinent resignation letter I shall soon send to the Agency's London Headquarters.

Please be advised that I have also decided not to concede to the Agency the rights of the book I have written at your suggestion in the form of a Black Bible which has fortunately taken a different form. If I finally decide to bring out the book, this will be done in due time and for purposes which neither you nor our employers would endorse.

I also consider it my duty to report that I fully acknowledge my financial obligations vis-a-vis the Agency and that I will pay the amount of £ 22.750 in the form of reparations. Let me remind you that this is the exact sum you had indicated during our last meeting, months ago, as my debt.

In closing, I would like to extend my regret for the fact that I have unwillingly caused you trouble, and my joy for finally being able to realize that every illness, regardless of how grave it may be, contains the elements of its own cure.

Sincerely,

Joseph Akritas

He closed the envelope and glued a stamp on it. Then he unlocked the trunk and took out the files with his best reports, two albums of photographs and a box of films and cassettes. A handful at a time, he took them to the bathroom and shoved them into the boiler.

In the trunk he left only the manuscripts for the "Other Side" and the recent material – photographs and films – he had drawn from in order to write the book.

At the top of the pyramid, inside the boiler, he piled all the certificates, awards and trophies he had garnered over a span of twelve years of work, then emptied a can of petrol over them.

He lit a match. A golden column blew out in front of him, broke in two and then, with a roar, turned black and rose high. He closed the boiler lid and took off his clothes. But the water was still cold, even though he had burnt the entire content of his trunk; and "of my old life" he added with a smile. He stepped out of the bathtub, put on his slippers, reopened the boiler and threw in logs and pine cones.

"They should produce greater and purer heat", he thought.

He soaped up indolently, meticulously, then surrendered to the rush of water. Never in his life had he enjoyed being drenched with hot, almost boiling water! Never before had he felt more relieved by a simple bath!

When he'd finished and walked out of the bathroom, he felt the urge to sing. He didn't know the words of even one song – though he loved music, he loved it more than she did, but he never told her that. He only knew fragments of verses and melodies. He smiled at his degradation, had a glass of cold milk, got dressed and walked to the study. He took the letter and was just about to leave the house, when he heard a car parking by the gate, followed by footsteps on the paved alley and a key turning. He walked to the middle door and saw her marching into the sunroom, confident and merry.

"Hello Joseph", she said with a casualness that was so like her, as if she had left home for school just that morning and was just now back for lunch.

"Hello Avgi", he replied in the same tone. "Good to see you".

He offered her a chair instead of a kiss or a handshake. Or the barrage of questions he had prepared, ages ago.

"Same here!"

She refused to sit down, opting to freshen up a bit and change clothes instead.

"Have you got any luggage? A suitcase?"

"That's all!" – a sports bag and a summer coat.

"Shall I make you a drink?"

"In a bit".

And she walked to the corridor.

"I'll go post a letter while you're settling in".

He left the house and set out for the grocer's. He met no one he knew on the way. He delivered the letter, bought fruit, vegetables and fresh milk.

When he returned home, she was still getting ready for her bath. He could hear her opening taps, walking to and from the bedroom, searching through closets, then heard the splash of her body sinking into the bathtub. She had been away for nine months and five days. And now that she was back, he could swear she had never left; only now she looked fresher and younger by nine months and five days.

It was a good thing she had come back today and not yesterday or the day before yesterday or at some time during the past trying week. If she had returned then, she wouldn't have said "Hello Joseph" as normally and casually as she had today. She would probably have said nothing, been at a loss for words, or even more likely, she would have held her peace trying to recognize him amongst the rubble; but today he was younger by three days, tomorrow by four. Maria's death and that of her child, rather than despair, had brought him peace.

She sat facing him, in her nightdress and gown.

"I feel restful after the bath", she said.

"Especially this one!" he stood up. "At some point I'll tell you how I heated the water. Are you hungry?"

"Thirsty".

He went to the buffet, took the clay goblets and filled them from the Archangielsks' demijohn.

"To your health!"

"To your health!"

They took a sip.

"Some more please", she kindly asked.

"Father Stavros claims it's spiked with drugs" he replied, refilling their goblets.

"Yes, but it's a harmless variety of drugs! I know the recipe. In fact, I'm now the owner of the distillery. They told me that once they had gone I would own everything!"

"They left on the day of the funeral. They stopped at the cemetery gate, they didn't attend the funeral procession or the internment. We buried her here".

"Yes, I know".

"The whole village walked with her chanting ululations and lamentations, and curses towards the 'culprits'. There was also a motley crowd from Nicosia. Many amongst them protested that her infant hadn't been buried with her. To appease them, Father Stavros promised to arrange for the corpse to be transported the soonest possible. I don't know what urged me, something stronger than logic, I couldn't keep it in check – I said there was no need for that. That it had already been done, both the transportation and the transfiguration. By that I meant of course... and I left before they'd lowered her body into the grave. As I exited the cemetery, I met them at the entrance. They told me they were 'happy for me'. I followed them; we returned to the village on foot, in silence. Outside the coffee shop, there was a taxi waiting for them. 'Him... Did you notify him?' I suddenly heard myself saying, though my initial decision was not to mention Michael at all. She spoke first: 'Yes, he knew!' – 'Yes, they know!' he added".

"They must know", Avgi said.

"There's been talk that it is they who burnt down the chapel. For Maria too, people say, they're to blame. For her death and for our child. For you too".

"Perhaps! In a way".

"How well do you know them?"

"As much as I've allowed myself to know them".

"What kind of human beings are they?"

"They're not exactly humans; they're of a different kind. They belong to another genus". She smiled, eyes on her wine. "Just as wine is not grapes and milk is not breasts".

"Yes; I'm only just beginning to suspect as much".

"To suspect or to understand?"

"They were the most inhuman couple I've ever met, in spite of their humanity!"

They emptied their glasses in prolonged silence. He decided to interrupt it. Bach was the most essential option he found. He put the record onto the pickup. The *moderato* brought about the exact opposite of that which he had intended: it made silence thicker and further solidified the mellifluousness in his solar plexus. Only now his thoughts took on easier and bolder shapes.

"She was ill. She died giving birth to ten buckets of blood and an explosion; in a rebirth of the entire world and me!"

Her expression betrayed knowledge and awareness.

"How do you know that?"

"Does it matter? The important thing is that it's done; it has been done since time immemorial…"

"And it was done unto us".

"Unto us!… Not for us!"

"For us too".

She smiled at him.

"What did you bring forth?" he asked her. "A human being or the Forerunner?"

"Must I have given birth too?" she said, looking behind her clay goblet into his eyes.

"You were away for exactly nine months. And five days".

"That's no proof".

"A few days more than she had needed to give birth and... die".

"I'm not dead!"

"You're not! Not yet or not as much as she is! Just as I haven't died as much as you have, not yet!"

He went back to the pickup and restarted the record that had been exhausted by pauses. Bach's cyan monologue resumed. Staccato.

"Can I make an assumption?" he asked her. "I'm not expecting verification".

They looked at one another.

"You fell gravely ill. The illness was the consequence of your health, as is the case with the few chosen ones. And you heard the echo of *Eros* resonating with you and you knew the life instinct was powerless in front of the formidable grave. At that precise moment in time they arrived at Spilia. You met them and at some point invited them over; they willingly accepted the invitation. They brought you their gifts, wine, fetishes, delicacies from their land. And a young man with a guitar or a flute.

And when you had finished your dinner, because they don't eat like we do, he started to play. You were swept away; and you spoke of the things we yearn to talk about but fear lest we become exposed, just as we're scared to act outside the context of general approval and tolerance. They said nothing, they would only listen, looking at the fireplace or the oddly glowing flowers or his chords. When you were done, you went to the bathroom and concluded your confession over the sink. Soon after that, she came to you with rosewater to dampen your forehead. And she led you back to the room, had you sit on the black armchair that's identical to the white one, their own, which now belongs to you, and he rose, stood by your side, as she stood by your other side, and the youth from the desert of the highlands came and stood before you, 'now that you're empty'. And he leant over you and kissed you in front of them. They flew out of the room and the house. You took your clothes off, threw them into the fireplace to burn, and he was naked too, always, without having to remove his clothes, or as if they burnt on his flesh as he wore them, and he approached and you opened up and let out a scream as if you were giving birth from that very moment. A few days or weeks later you discovered what would happen and made up your mind; not because you were scared but because they'd asked you to, within your emotional mind. They needed the setting for the new drama or the new Act; the stage had to be set for Joseph and Maria. You either went to Nicosia or followed him to Patmos, Cythera, Palestine, it doesn't matter where, and you gave birth to a son or blood or explosion. Or... They or others like Them collected it. As for your illness, it was healed during your pregnancy. The smaller within the larger. The greater always displaces the lesser".

He stopped talking.

"I neither confirm nor deny, as you have asked. However... Perhaps it was he who led me from the sink back to the room, and it was she who approached to kiss me. It is also possible that in a situation like this, when you stop dealing with humans and deal only with the essence of humans, the fecundation yields not a third person. It is also possible that nothing of the above has ever happened; nothing but something simpler or much more complex. Perhaps I left with him, on his Lilliputian boat, for their reservation by the River; perhaps I lived in their midst, amongst youngsters living the present as if they wouldn't be alive tomorrow, or as if they were already dead; or even as if they were going to live forever. I might have lived with them for nine months and five days and I might live for more or forever, until I eventually train myself to live as one who's about to die and at the same time as one who's immortal. And I might plan to go back there once I'll have settled everything pending.

"At the very moment she was breathing her last breath inside the operating room, I experienced the most redeeming orgasm; for the first time, just like those about to drown or be hanged. It was then I first suspected what it means exactly – copulation. It's self-sufficiency! And autotelism! Had it not been accompanied by an infusion of love, by a pressing feeling that I belonged to this world, that I was indebted to it… today I would be a rescued man. You are all set to leave and suddenly you realize you can't. You're obliged to be recruited, to wear the yoke, akin to a healthy cell, a therapeutic meniscus circling the wound; until when?"

"Until treatment comes!"

"Until death comes!"

"I'm not obliged to do it, nobody is".

"I know! And that's the worst thing, knowing that I'm not obliged, that I have the right to choose. The copulation I seek, I'm now well aware of that, is produced from making the most painful option; the supremacy of love over our much-desired freedom. There's the abominable truth! Loneliness is inexistent! It's the eclipse; only from our own point of view! Elsewhere there's the glow of light and warmth. We're the theoretical subdivisions, the geometrical combinations and the quotients of the Indivisible!"

"Therefore I have already been admonished! I am not as free as I assumed or as you suggested just now".

"I'm not, no. And you're not! We both shall be when one after the other we burst with health! Or when the planet bursts".

"And until then?"

"Until then we shall remain crucified within our glory, radiating within our sacrifice".

After a frugal supper they decided to walk in the woods.

Leaving the house, he reached out and held her hand. Her fingers willingly obeyed. He smiled at her. Her face glowed in the dusk.

From their yards and front doors, the neighbours looked at them astonished at their joy; disapprovingly. There was only one old lady, one they hadn't seen before, who greeted them by name, she said 'May you live long, my dears', and offered them peaches. Her timeworn face was well-shaped and noble, beautiful within its erosion. Her entire body, apart from the small face, was dressed in mourning.

"We'd better wash them", Avgi said. "They're sulphured".

They walked on, chatting; about the moist and pleasant scent of the earth and the orchards, about noon, when a sudden shower poured down, about fruit: the plums, peaches, apples and wild berries that weighed down the stems, fruit dense and silver-sprayed; about Father Stavros and Nicodemus who in the context of an interrogation lasting only a few minutes had confessed a "possible criminal negligence", just as Kyros Demetriades had done. Regarding the latter's transformation, that was as commented on as Maria's death. "And as commented on as your homecoming will be tomorrow!"

"When I saw our few neighbours gathering here after they caught sight of you this afternoon, to welcome you and ask where you'd been all this time, I remembered the day Maria was released from the clinic and they came here to greet her. What did you tell them? I was in the kitchen, I couldn't hear. By the time I returned with the sodas they had already begun to scatter".

"That I love them but what had taken place is only of my own concern. I'm healthy but tired and I'll make sure to call on all of them before I leave".

He turned to look at her.

"Yes, I'm leaving again. Once I sell the house and all my belongings, to invest in what's worthwhile".

"............"

"In guarded immoderation".

He hugged her; they walked on for a while without talking, their eyes gleaming in the half dark.

"There's a spring", Avgi said.

Even though the peaches weren't completely mature, still yearning for the sun, they ate them to their core. And they decided, on their way back, to walk into the first orchard they found and pick a few more for later that evening.

He told her of his decision to leave the Agency.

"Are you certain of what you're about to do?"

"I am today! As for tomorrow, I don't know. A while before you came, I burnt my old manuscripts and my entire archive. My 'successful' past. Yesterday it was the only thing I wanted to do, in order to devote myself to something else, something I can't as yet determine or define, to an impulse without a specific direction or goal... as yet. The truth is, these last few days I have often felt comical and displaced".

"Indeed you are, at times! What's important is that you've tasted the fruit of knowledge. If it's true that the Archangielsks have passed by the village, if it's true that Maria carried and bore the explosion that was to kill and heal her, if it's true that, at least for a fragment of a moment, you became of the same substance with this 'miracle', in between your comical crawling, you began to pace towards the rutty path". She went silent for a moment, before adding with a smile: "And it's more than obvious you've burnt those manuscripts in the boiler, that's why you're so cleansed! And there's this scent of a child or an infant about you! The truth is you're a comical, woeful, blind toddler in an unknown world that both enchants and scares you. In a world where you are both your mother and your father, indolent and helpless – and in front of you, instead of a future you have freedom that will lead you to sacrifice and redemption".

"Infantile life in my anti-world; in the plus that's really a minus!"

She squeezed his hand and asked:

"Are you afraid?"

"Yes! Of myself! Lest I falter".

A bat almost grazed their heads, left behind a trail of lack and began ascending into the dark sky.

"Have you noticed how awkwardly we have been talking?"

"When we may as well have kept our peace".

"There's an orchard".

They advanced bravely and filled their arms with fruit and branches in full bloom.

Back at the house, they saw two men waiting for them outside: the Principal and Moses Levy, a renowned Jewish journalist who had worked with Joseph at the Agency.

Demetriades, deeply moved, embraced Avgi, his "most distinguished friend and colleague" whose "disappearance had caused all of them terrible anxiety". He kissed her on both cheeks and exchanged courteous compliments with her. They agreed to meet at the soonest possible, to discuss the many important events that had transpired in Spilia during her absence and "if she so wished" share with him "which lucky mortals and blessed lands had enjoyed her presence for so many months".

They both apologized to Moses Levy for putting him 'on hold' — Joseph with the little Jewish he spoke, Avgi in French. As for Kyros Demetrides, he addressed the visitor in English, the only foreign language he had been able to learn 'more or less'.

"Mr Levy was absolutely adamant about meeting you", Demetriades apologetically told Joseph when the guest and Avgi proceeded to the living room. "I offered to bring him here".

"You did well! Just so you know, Moses Levy would dig me up anyway, even without your help".

"Indeed, he seems very intelligent!"

They walked to the living room, following the others. Moses Levy took a seat on the divan, Avgi opted for the black high-backed chair, and Joseph took the stool which he had dragged closer to the window.

"Why don't you sit, Kyros?" Avgi asked Demetriades who remained standing.

"I'd better take my leave!" he replied. "I'm sure you have things to talk about".

"First join us for a drink", Joseph suggested.

Demetriades acquiesced. "Alright, just one".

Joseph went to prepare the drinks and in the meantime suggested they spoke in English, the only language they could all manage.

When the glasses with the purple translucent wine of the Arch-angielsks were distributed, the three of them proposed a toast to welcome the visitor to Spilia and Cyprus.

"Thank you", Moses Levy replied and emptied his glass with a single gulp. "Lovely wine!" he said and licked his lips with the tip of his tongue. Then, he fixed his inquisitive, penetrating gaze on Akritas, adding: "Please, dear Joseph, accept my most profound and sincere condolences for your double loss". He said it in Yiddish, then translated the phrase in English, speaking in impeccable Oxford accent.

"Thank you", Joseph replied. In his voice, the observant visitor did not hear the tone that was 'appropriate' for the circumstances. It was a neutral voice.

But of course, Moses Levy offered no comment on what he'd seen and suspected. He changed the subject:

"I was just saying to Mr Demetriades that your village is the most beautiful and picturesque I've seen today as I travelled through the valley of Solea!"

"I had a slight objection", Demetriades offered. "I told Mr Levy there are much more beautiful and picturesque villages in Solea and in the adjacent valley of Marathasa, on the Southern slope of Troodos too! Spilia-Kourdali stands out for a different reason".

Joseph and Avgi listened without intervening.

"I have no reason to insist", Levy felt obliged to consent. "You know better, just as you know what it is that makes your village so unique. I do find it simply marvellous though! It's calm, picturesque, lavish green, devoid of exhaust emissions and Jews! Besides, it's the village of your choice!" And he looked at Joseph emphatically. "Perhaps this is what Mr Demetriades' clarification implied?"

His apt observation was left without reply.

Demetriades took advantage of the silence that had ensued the dialogue to finish his drink.

"I should be going!" he said and stood up.

He exchanged a warm handshake with the guest, said he would be happy to see him again and show him around the village, then walked to the front door. Avgi accompanied him. Before he left, they exchanged kisses again and confirmed their mutual wish to meet and talk in depth, before the villagers, joyful and extremely curious at her return, would lay siege on her.

In the living room, there was a long pause. Then, when Avgi returned, Moses Levy talked first, this time in a more formal, ceremonial tone.

"It has come to my attention, dear Joseph, that you have decided to resign from the Agency. I was truly sad to hear that!" he got straight to the point.

"Don't be sad, dear Levy. That particular decision had given me the greatest relief".

"Then, let me put it differently. I am sorry that the international mass media should do without you – if it's indeed true that you're not only abandoning your post at World News but the trade altogether, your... should I call it, your mission".

"You are well informed. But, trust me, I'm only just beginning to breathe freely again".

"If you say so... I must admit, it's readily obvious. You do look ten years younger; I do believe you, though this doesn't mean I also understand".

Avgi entered the room with a basket of fruit: apples, *pizzutello* grapes, peaches, cherries, the fruit they had picked during their afternoon walk, and other fruit she took from the fridge.

"How can I not insist on calling your region paradisiacal, with such fruit!" Levy remarked and filled his plate. "Even more so, when they're served by such a lovely lady!"

"Thank you", Avgi smiled.

"It is I who thank you, Miss. Had I not met you I wouldn't have reviewed my initial impression – that exceptional beauties are rare amongst Cypriot women! Thanks to you, I stand corrected and, mind you, this is no little thing for a strong-minded Jew! Are you by any chance non Cypriot?"

"I'm afraid I am Cypriot!"

They reached out to the fruit basket. Avgi helped herself to cherries, Joseph opted for a peach. They enjoyed them in silence, interrupted only by Moses Levy's knife slicing and meticulously peeling an apple.

"Though you speak words of praise for our fruit and region, I assume this is not where we owe the joy of your visit", Joseph broke the silence.

"Certainly not", the other man said. "Especially given my admission that I had no previous knowledge of these rare advantages!"

And he cast a meaningful look at Avgi. The young woman did not appear flattered by his persistent compliments. Politely she accepted them, but nonchalantly.

"So, what brings you here?" Joseph cut to the chase, almost curtly. "I mean Cyprus, Spilia".

"You! To both Cyprus and Spilia. I'm a guest of our common friend, Mr Serghides", and he finished his fruit.

"Would you like to talk in private for a while?" Avgi asked.

"Absolutely not!" Moses Levy said. "Everything that's going to be discussed here is of your concern too".

He wiped his hands, finished the wine that was left in his glass and settled into a more comfortable sitting posture. He looked at them in turn, made sure it was the right time to talk– "seriously", he added, "about facts and work". And he carried on: "We have been colleagues for years now and I take pride in considering we're also friends. Therefore, I will be clear and succinct. So! Neither the fruit nor the picturesqueness has brought me here! I came in order to obtain the most fascinating exclusive of my career!"

"Your manner leaves no doubt in my mind that you do not understand me", Akritas smiled.

"Precisely! How could I? You, the famous Joseph Akritas are offered this unique opportunity, you're practically served the news
of the century hot on a plate and instead of taking it, you so indolently lead an ascetic's life in Spilia!"

"Perhaps this is the price for what has been given me!" Joseph
calmly answered.

"Or, perhaps this is *my* chance! But we'll look at that as we pro-
ceed after both of you will have heard my offer - and taken it!"

"Are you sure we'll take it, whatever it might be?" Avgi spoke.

"This is what I believe and hope for! Aside from the moral gain
that will be credited to you, I have been authorized to offer this
too!"

He took two envelopes from his briefcase and placed them before them.

Their names were written on the envelopes in calligraphy: Mr
Joseph Akritas. Miss Avgi Josephides.

Avgi looked at Joseph inquisitively; he was looking straight ahead
with an expression that did not betray his reaction, or rather betrayed no reaction at all, of any kind.

"Perhaps we should first discuss your... immaterial gain?" Moses
Levy spoke again. "Yes? Wonderful! It will be nothing more than
utilizing the "GENESIS" topic and the quality guaranteed by my
own personal engagement. I pledge to process this overwhelming, unprecedented event so thoroughly that everything that's
bound to come out or be declared afterwards will be judged and
checked against my own version; that is to say, your own version,
Joseph! Because the seriousness I've already mentioned will be
grounded on the fact that every pertinent, unique element – the
extract of it all – shall be what you yourself will recount!"

He stopped talking and looked at them carefully. They were as detached as before he'd spoken, nonchalant. But he was undaunted, therefore he sought recourse in his second lure.

"Now let us come to the material gain. In the envelopes I have enclosed two cheques; twenty-two thousand Cyprus pounds made out to Mr Joseph Akritas, and ten thousand for Miss Josephides!"

He thought a long pause was necessary to bring out the dramatic quality of the moment and allow them to realize the extent of his offer.

"I find that the amounts you're proposing are extravagant for a story you could perfectly well obtain at very little expense – if any! As long as you leverage a few good contacts", Joseph Akritas said.

"Indeed! But, in truth, I could care less about the bare story, the contour which has become more or less known by now. Nor am I interested in the varied versions, rough diagrams and various assumptions that may be put forward by the second fiddles, the extras in this mystic drama. I'm interested in you! Your own experience, the catalysts that have – dare I say – transubstantiated you!"

"How did you learn of the small or big transfigurations that had followed the birth of the unseen?" Avgi asked. "None of this has been divulged!"

"But this is precisely why I make both of you this offer, dear Miss! To have them 'divulged' directly from you, through me! As for my sources, whence I have been informed of the premature efflorescence of the rose garden, the radiation secreted by objects that have been in close contact with the energy emitted during the 'labour' of the non being, the mysterious healing menisci, the post-mortem recuperation of Ms Akritas, the metamorphosis of

the gentleman who had accompanied me here – they are indeed
many. And according to what applies in journalism, they cannot
be disclosed". He turned to Joseph: "What do I want to learn
from you? First and foremost what has led you to the incompre-
hensible decision to abandon an amazing career? The hypotheses
published so far have failed to provide a convincing explanation,
at least one I myself, having known you quite well, would find
convincing. From the very start I thought something more serious was at work. There was this underground stream flowing, and
it would be so interesting to have it brought to the surface, to
quench the thirst of the thirsty who, mind you, are quite plentiful
in our time and age! Let us not hide; neither you nor I are free to
take decisions such as this, to abandon our *abri* for petty reasons
or, to speak as a journalist, for reasons that do not make for interesting news! Don't you agree? This is what my visit here aims at.
Interpreting the events which, let it be noted, are gradually accu-
mulating, gathering light, running in full swing. Indeed! The first
thing I was informed of upon my arrival in Cyprus was the death
of Ms Akritas. I rushed to the 'Hygeia' Polyclinic and whatever I
hadn't managed to extract from Dr Herodotou in my first head-
on attack, I learned from the nurse – without much effort mind
you. I merely convinced her that it was to her benefit to sell no
one but me what she knew about the case. After that, it was not at
all difficult to elicit and cross-check supplementary information
from the doctor and the other members of the Medical Council.
They all spoke 'in strict confidentiality' of course! Now that I've
mentioned Dr Herodotou, I'm sure you didn't know he had decided to put his career on the side for life, or for as long as it takes
him to investigate the causes of the amazing phenomena related
to your wife's pseudo-pregnancy, remedy and death – but above
all to discover what kind of 'amorphous' life or energy had been
secreted during the 'birth'; which of course was not a birth per
se but a mere splitting of the atom, an explosion, multiplication
to the nth power. In fact, he confided in me that he intends to seek

the help of all those who had recently come in contact with the deceased. He will see you, the nurses, his colleagues, the two foreigners and so on and so forth. I am convinced that that contact, rather the secreted energy, has brought on serious alterations of a biological nature, something like that, to all those exposed to it. This is what he intends to probe. In the meantime, the observations he's made so far have given rise to a few pieces of evidence bound to cause a stir and a schism in the international scientific community. Needless to point out that Dr Herodotou is a scientist of great acclaim! Anyway, that's a different story. At a second stage, and always in strict confidentiality, I obtained additional information, of a different nature, from your family physician, Dr Evangelou, and later on by your parish priest, a man called Stavros! I must say Mr Stavros had eagerly wished to impress me with various theories about the Archangielsks and the young men they had invited here, as well as the methods they would apply to seduce their victims. To have a complete image, I also spoke to the area's police sergeant, and to your former help: a girl named Rodi who, I'm sure you know had served as a kind of Trojan horse for the priest! Another supporting actor and one I haven't yet managed to lure into making a confession or putting forward different theories, is the gentleman who had accompanied me here a while ago. I decided not to pressure him for the time being. After all, I believe that only you can salvage my inquiry from the impasse it has been led to in the area of the absurd. Only you can provide a reasonable or verisimilar explanation and that personal and human quality that will elevate it to a major revelation, an embarkation upon something new!"

He turned to Avgi:

"And you, Miss! Your case is extremely interesting too. Your mysterious disappearance, its duration and the exact time of your return, your relations with the Archangielsks and their young guest, this odd relay race! I do believe you have been the prelude to the same story, the introduction to the main theme, if I'm allowed the metaphor!"

Silence fell again, for a while. Then, Moses Levy asked:

"Could I please have some more of the wine of the Archangielsks? This is what you've served just now, correct? I've heard so much about it..."

Akritas offered him a goblet. Moses Levy discreetly sniffed it before bringing it to his lips. Eyes fluttering, he tasted the wine.

"Odd!" he said. "Interesting! And, just like most things, it lacks meaning".

"Perhaps everything lacks meaning!" Joseph smiled. "And perhaps this is precisely what makes it all 'interesting' in your own words. Then again, it could be that the meaning escapes us".

"Hardly", Moses Levy answered. "You have the key. Miss Avgi has the spare key. The key, my dear, is your own experience, your own version of the events! From the very start down to the dramatic climax!"

He went silent for a while, then:

"This certainty of mine is enhanced by the fact that the dramatis personae are none other than you and the deceased. You too, Miss Anna! Indeed, I have been informed that 'Avgi' is the name you've adopted long after your baptismal. Joseph, Mary and Anna! Anna, the name your godfather, Akritas' father, gave to you".

"Is this the line you intend to follow?"

"For the time being! Unless you share with me new and more intriguing perspectives".

"What do you believe, as a person I mean?"

"My role is limited to phrasing the myth and creating a suggestive ambiance; to exploiting raw material and, above all, recording your experiences, as I've already said. And this I intend to
do with the precision and impartiality that characterize Maria's
notes on the wall-paintings! By the way, have you read them?"

"No! They were left at the chapel. They're probably burnt".

"A mister Nicodemus had picked them up, just as he did with
the drawings. I obtained everything for just thirty pounds! They
provide two fine testaments, and also wonderful specimens of an
anxious, might I add, writing effort. And the sketches, they're
genius! I would be willing to pay several thousands to get hold
of them".

Joseph got up and stood by the window. He was completely still,
looking outside. He said hello to a passer-by with whom he went
on to exchange a few phrases: "Yes!" – "..." – "No, she came back
yesterday! You will see her at some point" – "..." – "They left" –
"..." – "Us? No, we're already their past!" – "..." – "Or perhaps
they are our future!" – "..."

Then he turned back to face Moses Levy:

"Did you really think I would sell you this story? That I would be
willing to exploit it?"

"Indeed I did! Perhaps in order to safeguard your new role. It
appears you've already taken up a role which excludes self-
promotion; it even excludes the promotion of your own ideas.
You either belong or want to belong to that category of men for
whom only the others write or speak. Men who are perhaps not
allowed to..."

He finished his wine.

"I truly find it interesting!" he said, without clarifying what he meant. Then: "Well? Have I convinced you?"

"..."

"Miss?"

"I'm sorry!"

"Are you forbidden from above to say yes?"

"We're not forbidden anything, no one intervenes in our decisions", Joseph answered. "The reason I don't speak is because I'm not yet in a position to do so. I wish I could! I suppose I have the necessary senses, that are just beginning to awaken, and a few limited experiences – that may be useful for the role you've implied, if it's a new role I will someday be obliged to play. But for these as yet few, very few things, I lack the words. Perhaps there aren't any words to describe them".

"Do you mean that if I decided to wait there would be hope?"

"Maybe! But I know you won't be able to wait, not for as long as required".

"Wouldn't you want to try? I will ponder on everything you will have told me, delve into it exhaustively, to your full satisfaction. Miss Avgi's too. We will cooperate upon this condition".

"It would be pointless and impossible, Moses my friend!"

"In other words, instead of the explanation, either partial or complete, that you and Miss Avgi could offer me, you opt for misinterpretation and distortion? That's absurd! I'm only saying that because I know you are not naïve to believe that this whole story will be kept forever secret, between you two or between your doctors. It is a story, and forgive me for phrasing it as clumsily, that's much bigger than you! Even the story as such, its proper shell! If you two agreed to help me, the truth wouldn't suffer any distortions. I'm sure you know I would not hesitate to attempt, by lack of other interpretations, to provide my own or those expected and required by the readers. It is you who will push me to this desperate solution. And, of course, other faults will follow. Because I intend to do what I've just described using as much experience or skill I possess. But my articles will only be the beginning; the sparkle. Others will be intrigued, perhaps too many others... They will hunt you down, dozens of our well-known or unknown colleagues will pressure you, and I'm not talking only about professionals like ourselves, but the paparazzi and the sensationalists and everyone seeking to exaggerate their own conclusions or what they feel will be more appealing to the public. Once news of this unexplainable birth leaks, people will start hunting you two, the indirect carriers of mystic, 'healing' energy that had been secreted, and then hordes of un-cured patients will rush in asking for talismans, fetishes and in-stant treatments with menisci and radiation, followed by censors and zealots, the gullible and the sarcastic ones, the vengeful and the tranquil... But you know all this. Now don't tell me you'd rather have the semi-ignorant ones and the opportunists explain or customize everything due to the absence of a solid, authentic standard that only your truth and Miss Avgi's can provide. Don't tell me you prefer Babel to the New Bible!"

"I have no preference. Nor am I capable of stopping you or them or what's about to come. In the same way you are not capable of writing the 'New Bible according to Akritas' quid pro quo. After all, what does this even mean — the 'New Bible'? If you're trying to specify what this experience has added to or taken from me, you try in vain. The square minds of this era have no wish to buy the god-possessed absurd".

"Is this your final answer?"

"It is for now".

"Very well then! I will insist no further", Moses Levy gave in. He stood, briefcase underarm, ready to collect the two envelopes too.

"Where do you intend to spend the night?" Joseph asked. "It's rather late to return to Nicosia".

"I'm sure I'll find a hotel or a guesthouse, either in the village or somewhere near here".

"You can stay with us. There's an extra room with a bed available".

"Is there any hope too?"

They dined casually in the kitchen: salami, cold chicken, *myzithra* and wine. They ate with appetite and euphoria which, as time passed, Moses Levy felt maturing between the other two to a secret attraction, a rapport he ignored, one that excluded without belittling him. "So, back there again!" – "Yes!" – "To the River of immoderation!" – "Don't forget its second bank, the one I need you to describe for me some day". – "Where are you planning to travel to?" – "Where I haven't been yet: Cythera and Patmos!"

Once they finished their supper, Moses Levy, looking for something to say or do, offered to do the dishes.

"But of course! We'll all help", she said.

They methodically arranged inside the fridge what had been left on the table and stood by the sink. Joseph soaped the plates, Avgi rinsed them and Moses wiped them dry. "There, do you share?" – "Everything!"

They went back to the living room. The two envelopes were still on the table, half-opened and intact. They sat down, she on the divan, he next to her, on the ground. Moses Levy sat on the armchair facing the window. A light scented breeze blew, causing the improvised candelabra to tremble and drizzle amidst their silence. Twenty minutes without a single word!

"I've really overstayed my welcome!" Moses Levy felt the need to speak.

"Not at all!" Joseph replied. "Nevertheless, so that you won't feel bad, I assure you that your presence will not prevent us from being what we are..."

"We'd be even more comfortable if you too felt the same, Moses", she added.

"That would be rather difficult", Moses Levy smiled with relief and wonder at her amical tone.

"Oh come on! Even small children can do this".

"Then I was right to say this would be rather difficult. I do promise I'll try though..."

He unfolded his newspaper as quietly as he could. Then he entrenched himself behind her in order to focus on his reading. It was both pointless and hypocritical. The only thing he was interested in was them and the impregnated relation he could sense between them, somewhat erotic, he thought. Perhaps this wasn't irrelevant with what had transpired or was still at work. Their silence, their rejection of his offer, was one more reason for him to summon all his powers in order to decrypt their affair and make the best of the chance they had offered him, to spend a few more hours under the same roof with them.

Perhaps... But listen, they're talking:

Census 243

"…the record I brought".

"Yes, I'm waiting!"

She went to the sunroom to pick up her leather bag from the chest where she had left it upon her return. From inside the bag she took an untitled 45 rpm record, its cover colourful and smooth, a sun clock wrinkled by the shadows of dozens of suns. On the reverse, a lotus or a gull against a deeply cyan background.

She carefully unsheathed the record and walked to the pickup.

A bird squeak in a lull. Flute and piano; rather, guitar. A dialogue between a wind, percussion and string instruments; yes, definitely a string instrument. Feathers fluttering, spread over a surface of rhythms during tide, converging and growing in the company of illegible voices and primal instruments.

… and the stylus hovering over the black surface akin to an artificial arm either blessing or legislating…

Looking at the red magnetic axis of rotation, she stood still, the record spins flickering in her eyes, sky-blue and yellow… and again… She inhaled… exhaled… Again… stirring and unfolding one arm. Slowly, as if she was coming out of a coma. Then, the second arm, upwards and backwards, more spasmodically, akin to the metallic stylus of the pickup, lending the body a circular impulse. Slowly again, upstream of the music; one in two, as if she was struggling with plastic movements against the flow of the river or sinking into the weightless space, bound to a secret thread that allowed her only one movement forward, then back again. A single movement and back again.

...he clapped his hands. Again. Clunked his heel. Harder. Then a step ahead, two on the spot, towards her.

...bending at the waist, she was rolling and sliding without moving her feet; one arm hovering, free, the other extended perpendicularly as if fixed to the roof by another, invisible hand.

....a step again, two on the spot, his body erect like a sword; never again had he danced as loosely, promptly, allowing his trunk, arms, legs and head a pace faster than the music's – two in one, lift, lift and place.

...they convened...

...he placed his arm around her waist and lifter her up.

...they were united.

...they slipped into one another.

...the two heteronyms became one and the same.

...with the shriek of a bird or a flute.

The whole house was the colour of sky-blue in the kingdom of the gull or lotus, replete with agile shadows like the sun clock of the reverse side.

She gently took his hand and placed it on her cheek; then on her breast. They stopped. So did the music. They told him: "You can stay for as long as you like or dance or sleep; both the room and your bed are ready". And they walked away together, embraced, towards Maria's room.

Moses stood there, still, holding the newspaper that all of a sudden was rid of its meaning, its words and aims and anaemic parables washed off by the music and dancing and the emitted colours; rid of everything other than what now unfurled before his eyes, big and trivial, promise-laden and hollow.

He played the other side on the pickup, loud, so as not to hear what was happening behind the door.

It was a deep voice, a single phoneme, a cappella, and mute, blurred, rising in waves from an empty human tube under a relentless sun that killed every shadow and hope.

He'd spent half the night awake, listening to the great Erotic from their rooms. It carried on for hours, even after they had separated, retired to their own rooms – he was certain they had separated, he saw them walking past him when, panicked, he rushed back to his room.

"Goodnight".

And then, suddenly, an unknown word as if of pain or blessing, like an invocation, and uncanny sounds; deific mantras, words fragmented like primal cries or supplications or contracted between them, and amalgamated concepts that within the potent moans of the two in the two rooms should have, must have had a deeper meaning, their proper sense and causality that now escaped him.

He yielded to the strong impulse, his doubt-discarding addiction. Quietly he opened his bedroom door. On his toes he walked down the hallway, near the two now closed bedrooms on either side of the corridor. From her room, a persistent redemptive panting – or was this the wrong word? Slow, half as slow than that of the panting from his room. And their new, second synaeresis with what was beyond their bodies, relentless.

The following morning, as he was about to leave, they handed him the two envelopes.

"That means..."

"Yes!"

He reached out his hand to shake theirs.

"Let me say again that what I choose to write tomorrow will be what I sincerely believe. And I do hope and wish you never regret not confiding in me last night".

"But we spent the whole night talking to you, dear Moses!"

Excerpts from reviews

Frangiski Ambatzopoulou PhD, *University Professor, Writer, Literary Critic.*

Excerpt from an essay published in the "Athens Review of Books" in May 2014.

[...] In this strongly enigmatic and symbolic novel we follow the life of a famous war correspondent, Joseph Akritas, and his wife, Maria, the two of them having retreated to a mountainous village of Cyprus, namely Spilia (or Kourdali), known for the Byzantine wall-paintings decorating its church. Joseph was led to the village by disillusionment surrounding his work –the conviction that the Mass Media turn the tragedy of war into a spectacle – and by a need for authenticity. The solution is provided through a myth personified by the co-protagonists: the archaeologist couple, the Archangielsks, and young Michael of Patmos – all three representative of emblematic personae from the ranks of the "angels". From Michael's coupling with Maria, a new divine power shall be borne, explosive energy emerging from the archetypical mother, and spreading into the environment, either directly or indirectly affecting and benefitting everything. It is the kind of energy that liberates, heals, purifies and transforms anyone within its range or anyone truly seeking it. The reporter Joseph Akritas shall not hesitate to burn his entire archive compiled of onsite reports across the Third World. By contrast, other characters, such as the village priest, shall prove unready to receive the benevolent energy and shall remain captive within the circle of the demons of doom.

[...] A desperate effort to tear apart realistic representation, *Census* draws inspiration from the source of the meta-psychical, mystic worldview. Imbued with a prophetic dimension, given the time when it was written, this genre of fiction struggles to find affinities with other works of the same period in Greece – perhaps *Angelica's Dreams* (1958) by Eva Vlami could be one such work. Closer affinities are found in the magic realism of Latin American authors, for instance the short story "A very old gentleman with enormous wings" by Gabriel Garcia Marquez, or Isabel Allende's novels. The trademark of magical realism as opposed to other genres of imaginative literature is the matter-of-fact inclusion of magical elements in an otherwise completely realistic setting.

Yiogros Kehayoglou PhD, University Professor, Writer, Literary Critic

"Nea Epochi" Magazine, Issue 31, Summer 2009

[...] Today we could add that the author's delving (familiar from many of his other works) into Gnosticism, esotericism and the more familiar or exotic mystic and mythological structures of the Near and Middle East and of Far Asia, equips Cypriot literature with an innovative novel that significantly predates Umberto Eco's or Dan Brown's composite or "bestselling" achievements and is conjoined with neoteric writing, originating not only from the movement of low-key, suggestive symbolism, but also from the 20th century's modernisms. And it does so without ever betraying the main need for the gist of the plot, in other words for the piece of meat that, in T.S. Elliot's words, a writer threw to the vigilant lions keeping guard outside – namely the appetite of the "average reader" – when wanting to break into a castle or a soul. There's something more interesting to add about the writing ethos of P. Ioannides: that neither the need to unravel the action thread smoothly and enticingly (the "time full of wonder, time sown with magic") nor the concern to render the narration's inner, esoteric and autobiographical-confessional aspects in a satisfactory and comfortable manner, sway the author into forgetting his enduring sharp, dissociative, even satirical and reprimanding gaze over the social surroundings and over "representative" types of Cypriot reality and actuality. [...]

Andreas Christophides, Literary Critic, Essayist, Poet

Excerpt from the Preface to the second edition, Ledra Publications, Athens

[...] The absurd that envelopes Ioannides is acquired.

At the heart of darkness the writer discovers White. A White that cannot relate to humans as they play dice - *pessoi*, stuck in the mire of a planet befouled by them.

The absurd becomes intertwined with the god-possessed, the *entheon*. If you will, it becomes invalidated by the *entheon*.

Coexisting alongside the descent Ioannides endeavours into the deep end of the age of the murderers, is the transcendence of a secret that receives, in spite of everything the observer sees and records, in spite of the biddings of Logic, a Notional Universe that coats Dirt.

Today there's talk of meta-themes in Science.

Author Panos Ioannides, in "Census", offers his own meta-physical meta-theme. Is it incidental that absolute mathematic harmony, the recurring internal rhythm of Bach's world, imbues the pages of the book? I don't think so. Nothing in Ioannides' novels is ever random or redundant.

Where, in the book, the miracle is either gestated or delivered in the mythical sense of the term, Panos Ioannides' discourse literally takes off.

Concise, elliptical sentences, the seemingly simplified wording (from a master) are put aside to make room for a language that endeavours to serve as a figure of extra-logical and extra-worldly transcendences. Eloquence, in the best possible meaning of the term, accompanies those passages of the book where cosmic drama cedes its place to metaphysical mystery.

With "Census", Panos Ioannides does not merely find his meta-theme; through it he carries us outside the comedy of manners of a specific place (in Balzac's interpretation of *comédie de moeurs*) to secret contemplation that rises above the tragedy of a world gone astray.

Andreas Kounios, *Journalist, Literary critic*

"Alithia"Daily, 15. 1. 2011

Bold. Heretic. Potent like a punch in the gut. But above all, perceptive. A novel of rare literary and philosophical aesthetic, written in 1973 by Panos Ioannides who, here too, demonstrates writing and imaginative expertise. Let me say it from the start: "Census" is a difficult novel. Its twists and turns are mind-boggling, they cause disbelief; but once the initial layer of dust settles, you can go on and relish the flow of the narration which is replete with unworldly dimensions and a miracle that splinters the reader to the very core.

[...] Even those passages the average reader may find vague, obscure, almost unreal – they too radiate through the author's descriptive vigour. Panos Ioannides, in the year 1973, is proclaimed a prophet, a raconteur of events that can only stem from inconceivable imagination. And still, behind the profoundly philosophical, religious might I add, subplot of the novel, the writing of Panos Ioannides flows clear and fresh like water from a spring.

Anthos Lykavgis, *Journalist, Poet, Literary Critic*
"Phileleftheros" Daily, 9.1.1974

[...] According to an Oriental saying, man receives as much light from a text as he has within him. This is absolutely true of "Census", where the reader-observer does not know which of the projecting climaxes of the narration comprises the ultimate message.

[...] Panos Ioannides is established as an excellent artisan of composite plot. But he never stays there. Rising above the logic of things, he leaps into metaphysics. Still, he doesn't "do" metaphysics, though they are present in surreal situations structured throughout by logical consistency. His aim is not to validate any metaphysical theories but to bring his symbols to maturity, endow them thus with new dimensions.

Yorgos Lysiotis, *Essayist, Literary Critic*
"Phileleftheros" Daily, 25.3.1975

[...] As the plot unfolds, the writer's voice becomes all the more tense, asthmatic, fragmented, as words are reduced to unconscious fragments, and associations become ruptured alongside logical cohesion and the elucidation of meanings. The author fully achieves his goal, setting the reader against inner speculation, an agitation of the Ego that commences from the background of the unconscious and terminates in subjective human conscience. His voice is graced with solid psychological poise and unique sharpness of the spirit equivalent to a surgical scalpel. On the whole, Panos Ioannides ranks amongst the leading representatives of modern prose in Cyprus and the wider Greek area.

About the author

Panos Ioannides was born in Famagusta, Cyprus, in 1935. He studied Mass Communications and Sociology in the USA and Canada. He served as Director of Radio and Television Programmes at the Cyprus Broadcasting Corporation. He has been writing literature, mostly prose and theatre, since 1955. Works of his have been translated

photo © Eleni Papadopoulou

and published in their entirety or in parts in French, German, English, Russian, Romanian, Chinese, Hungarian, Polish, Serbo-Croat, Turkish, Persian, Bulgarian, Swedish, and other languages. His plays Gregory, Peter the First, The Suitcase, and Ventriloquists have been staged in Greece, England, USA and Germany. He served as Chairman of the Cyprus Theatre Organization (ThOK) Repertory Committee, and as President of the Cyprus PEN Centre. He lives in Nicosia, Cyprus.

Short stories and novellas by Panos Ioannides have been published in the following anthologies and magazines:

SHORT STORY INTERNATIONAL, New York, Issues 60, 62 and 98

SUDDEN FICTION, World short story anthology, Norton and Co, New York-London, 1992

THE STORY TELLER, International Prose Anthology, Edition Nelson, Canada, 1992

FOREIGN LITERATURE, Cyprus Prose Anthology in Chinese, Beijing 1988

ZYPRISCHEN MINIATUREN, Romiosini Publications, Cologne, 1987

KALIMERHABA, Trilingual Cyprus Prose and Poetry Anthology in German, Greek and Turkish, Romiosini Publications, Cologne, 1992

CIPRUSI GOROG ELBESZELESEK, Cyprus Anthology in Hungarian, Europa Konyukiado Publishing, Budapest, 1985

PROSE AND POETRY, Hellenica Chronica Publ., Paris 1993

GRIEKENLAND AAN ZEE, Anthology of Greek Literature in Dutch, Chimaira Publishing, Groningen, Holland, 2001

LITERATURA DE LA ISLA DE CHIPRE, Anthology in Spanish, University de la Playa Ancha, Chile, 2003

GREEK WRITERS TODAY, Volume I, Hellenic Authors Society Publ.

He has been awarded five National Prizes for Literature by the Cyprus Ministry of Education and Culture for his works.

CYPRUS EPICS, short stories, 1968

CENSUS, Novel, 1973

THE UNSEEN ASPECT, short stories, 1979

THE UNBEARABLE PATRIOTISM OF P.F.K., novel, 1989

KOAZINOS, novel, 2012

Prizes awarded for his theatrical plays:

GREGORY, 1st Prize at the 5th International Theatrical Festival, Sofia, 1976

ONESILUS, 1st Prize of the Cyprus Society of Playwrights, 1980

DRY MARTINI, 1st Prize of Cyprus National Theatre Organization, 1984.

In 1992 Panos Ioannides was awarded the «Theodosis Pierides and Tefkros Anthias» Prize for his contribution to Cyprus Literature.

In 2007 he won the highest award given by the Cyprus Ministry of Culture to a writer: Merit Award for Letters and the Arts.